She tried to pack away her dreams of a family.

Locked the wish up tight in an old chest in her heart and tossed the key. The days of hoping for a husband and longing for children were gone.

Yet in the car, listening to Kellen and his girls, the dream almost felt attainable again. If she couldn't have a family of her own, perhaps she could grow old next door beside Skylar and Ruthy. Sure, it wouldn't have the marriage part. A man like Kellen would never settle for a woman like her.

Maggie stole a glance his way.

He looked over at her again. Their stares collided and Maggie's breath caught. Kellen was handsome. Ten times more handsome than any of the other men in Goose Harbor. And then there was that voice…

"Sing with us, Maggie." He winked again.

"I…I don't know the song." Her gaze broke with his and skittered to look out the window.

That was the crux of everything, wasn't it? *I don't know the song.* What did she know of love and romance?

Jessica Keller is a Starbucks drinker, avid reader and chocolate aficionado. Jessica holds degrees in communications and biblical studies. She is multipublished in both romance and young-adult fiction and loves to interact with readers through social media. Jessica lives in the Chicagoland suburbs with her amazing husband, beautiful daughter and two annoyingly outgoing cats who happen to be named after superheroes. Find all her contact information at jessicakellerbooks.com.

Books by Jessica Keller

Love Inspired

Goose Harbor

The Widower's Second Chance
The Fireman's Secret
The Single Dad Next Door

Home for Good

Visit the Author Profile page at Harlequin.com for more titles.

The Single Dad Next Door

Jessica Keller

HARLEQUIN® LOVE INSPIRED®

Recycling programs
for this product may
not exist in your area.

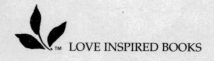 LOVE INSPIRED BOOKS

ISBN-13: 978-0-373-87971-7

The Single Dad Next Door

Copyright © 2015 by Jessica Koschnitzky

www.Harlequin.com

Printed in U.S.A.

And hope does not put us to shame, because God's love has been poured out into our hearts through the Holy Spirit, who has been given to us.
—*Romans* 5:5

For Sadie, who, upon reading the first chapter of *The Widower's Second Chance* (the first book in the Goose Harbor series), immediately asked when we'd hear Maggie's story.

Chapter One

A car door slammed outside, jolting Maggie West awake.

Like tugging a quilt to cover her body on a cold morning, she yanked on the edge of her dream in an effort to fall back to sleep again. She closed her eyes tightly and tried to force herself to rest a little longer. Being the manager of the West Oaks Inn, she so rarely had the opportunity to stay in bed past five in the morning. Under normal circumstances, she'd be in the kitchen right now, whipping up her latest gourmet creation for her guests. But she currently had no guests despite many schools being on spring break.

Tomorrow morning there would be guests to feed, but she'd prepared their rooms last night. She'd still go over the rooms one last time today before people arrived tonight, but for once, her plan had been to stay under her covers for most of the morning.

So much for that idea.

Oh well, eight in the morning was sleeping in long enough for her. Maggie let her eyes adjust to the bright light streaming in through her lace curtains. Her room was a mishmash of antiques, country charm and hand-me-downs. And she liked it that way. The sheet of glass that covered the top of the hundred-year-old dresser near the closet had once been

the top counter of a pharmacy. She often tried to picture
the people who had leaned against that counter to look at
what was inside the case. Had they been sick people buying
leeches? Or children with their noses pressed into the glass
begging for the penny candy inside?

That was the joy of old things. They told stories. Each
piece held a history worth remembering. Half the furniture that filled the rooms in the inn were pieces she'd saved
from the curbside—stuff others were going to throw away.
People were so set on making things modern or redesign-
ing perfectly functional homes. They lost sight of the wonder of remembering days long ago when life was slower.
Safer. Better.

She rolled onto her side and stared at her nightstand. The
old trunk set on its narrow end had belonged to her grandmother and still smelled like Gran's lilac lotion whenever
Maggie opened it up. On top of the makeshift nightstand
rested her cherished family heirlooms—her father's favorite timepiece, the brooch her mother had always worn to
church, as well as a photo of her sister, Sarah. All people
who had left the world—*left her*—far too early.

Now she'd have to find something of Ida's to place there.
Maggie rubbed her palm over the ache in her chest.

Seeing those belongings each morning made her feel
a little less alone. She knew their owners were gone but
cherished remembering them all the same.

"Why'd you have to go, Ida? Why?" Maggie sat up in
bed and pressed her fingers against her eyes. Maggie had
revisited that day a month ago a hundred times in her mind,
wondering if there was some way she could have saved her
elderly neighbor. But the doctor said the heart attack had
been quick. *Too quick*. That nothing could have been done
to change things.

Once again, Maggie had been powerless to help the people she loved. At least now there was no one left to fail.

Ida Ashby hadn't been related to Maggie by blood, but the bond had been just as strong. For the past couple years Ida had been the only family she had left after Caleb, her late sister's widower, had remarried.

She couldn't focus on her losses anymore. Taking stock would only depress her. Maggie refused to let herself feel that way. Besides, thinking about Ida brought to light the fact that the very room she was lying in at the moment might no longer belong to her. Not that it belonged to her in a monetary sense, but Ida had let her stay in the residential portion of the inn even though Ida owned it. What if the new owner kicked her to the curb?

Stop. Thinking like that would lead to no good.

Flopping back onto the pillows, she tugged her blanket to her chin again and scrunched her eyes shut. She pulled back her dream—the one she'd had a thousand times since high school. Okay, she wasn't asleep again—it was too late for that—but she could picture everything as if she were.

Wearing a white, flowing dress, she stood barefoot in a valley as an army of dark characters stalked toward her. Her dream self let out a scream. As usual, a man riding a white horse, brandishing a sword, appeared at the top of the hill. Turning his steed, he charged down the steep cliff and leaned over to effortlessly scoop Maggie up into his arms and carry her away from danger. Every inch of her felt alive. She was safe in the arms of her hero—her knight in shining armor.

Just like always, he rode with her to a field of wildflowers and then slowed his horse. Slipping down, he gathered her in his arms and set her on the cool earth. Maggie leaned forward to lift up his helmet, to offer him a kiss.

Outside the inn, another car door slammed.

"No! No!" Maggie moaned, releasing the pillow she was snuggling with. In the years the dream had reoccurred, not once had she seen the face of her rescuer. *If only...*

Maggie shook that thought away and finally shoved out of bed.

Prince Charming was never coming. For the first few years of her thirties, she'd joked that he was only lost along the way to finding her and—so like a man—wouldn't ask for directions. But Maggie had long stopped repeating that line. It hurt knowing that not even a lost prince was coming, but there it was. She might as well get used to the imaginary man in the shiny helmet, because he would be the only champion she'd ever have.

Voices sounded outside. They were closer than people walking on the sidewalk, which meant she possibly had drive-by business and someone wanted to book one of the open rooms for tonight.

Shoving her blinds apart, she squinted out the window. No vehicles were parked in the small lot in front of the inn. But then, where?

Her vision narrowed in on a green Subaru wagon parked in front of the home next door—Ida Ashby's cottage. The home had stayed empty since her funeral. No one at the wake had known whom she'd left her house to, and Maggie had been too afraid to ask—fearing that knowing would lead to her being evicted from the inn quicker. And that couldn't happen.

She fisted her hands.

The old West Mansion should be hers. After all, Maggie was the only West left. As a member of the town's founding family, she should have a right to the home. Even if she couldn't afford the place. When she almost lost it, Ida had swooped in and saved her. Ida purchased the mansion and proposed the idea of a bed-and-breakfast, offering to let

Maggie live in a portion that would be converted for residential use and run the place. Most people in Goose Harbor still thought Maggie owned the place, and Ida hadn't minded them assuming that. With Maggie's culinary background, it had been the perfect solution.

Would the new owner announce that she was basically a squatter? It would ruin her reputation in town. *Poor Maggie. All her family is gone and she couldn't even hang on to her inheritance.*

Maggie hadn't been invited to the reading of the will, but she knew Ida hadn't left the inn to her. She'd been foolish to assume Ida would. Ida had family to give her things to—even if that family had never visited her. Even if Maggie had been the one to take care of Ida every day since Mr. Ashby had passed away. A lawyer showed up on Maggie's doorstep a week after the funeral and told her she was allowed to stay…for now. That was it.

Real comforting.

Why hadn't she been saving money for an event like this? With not much in her savings, she didn't have many options if she was told to vacate the inn. If she hadn't given her money…

She shook her head. Thinking of *him* wouldn't help. It never did.

Her hair probably looked fearsome. Thirty-some odd years of life hadn't been long enough to learn how to tame her curls. No matter. She would just pin it here and there and put on some jeans and head over to meet whoever was in Ida's home. Perhaps they were just stopping in to check on the place. Or maybe they'd turn her out on the street the instant they met her.

On second thought…her bed still looked like a pretty good place to spend the day.

No. *Be strong. Put on a brave face. Like always. Don't let them see fear.*

She needed to stop hiding.

She needed to see how bad her future was about to become.

Kellen Ashby couldn't stop groaning.

When the lawyer contacted him to say he'd inherited all of his aunt's belongings—including her home in the picturesque tourist town of Goose Harbor—he'd envisioned something grander than a cottage. Much grander. The squatty house with its low ceiling looked as though it belonged on the set of the movie *The Hobbit*. Rounded front door included. Thick vine plants snaked over the side of the house and up onto the roof. If he took a machete to those, would they grow right back? Being raised in Arizona and then living in Southern California gave him little experience when it came to vine tending. Or any sort of greenery, come to think of it.

What had he gotten himself into?

Kellen scrubbed his hand down his face.

Would moving to Michigan just be one more mistake in his life? First rejecting the upbringing and religion of his parents, and then leaving home with his band to tour. The parties.

He shook his head.

The groupies—at least the one. *Cynthia.* Trusting that she cared about him had been his biggest mistake. She'd wanted his money. Wanted the fame that was within the band's grasp. But not him. And not their daughters, either.

How could a woman walk out on her children? He'd never understand that.

Yes, there was a lot of wrong in his past. But two years ago when he finally gave up trying to live up to the world's standards and instead, gave himself over to God—the mistakes had been washed away.

Right?

He fisted his hands.

Goose Harbor wasn't a mistake. It was a provision. Plain and simple. Aunt Ida had no reason to leave her possessions to him, so the events had to be what his brothers always called a *God thing*.

Honestly he couldn't remember what Aunt Ida even looked like. A picture inside would hopefully solve that mystery for him. He'd met the woman twice in his life. Both of those times had been in his childhood before he took off from home right after his eighteenth birthday.

His three brothers had questioned why their aunt had left him everything and hadn't mentioned them in the will. But Kellen had no answer for them. He hadn't kept in touch with her. Hadn't thought about her over the past twelve years. Not once.

Yet here he stood on her property—now his property.

"Dad! This place is so cool." Skylar, his oldest, rushed past him and yanked open the door. Her light red, crooked pigtails bobbed as she darted inside. She peeked her head back out the door again. "Do you think the Seven Dwarves lived here? It looks like their home, doesn't it? Like the pictures in my book. Don't you think so, Ruthy?" Skylar grabbed hold of her younger sister's chubby hand and gently led her inside.

Kellen took a deep breath. He could make the tiny cottage work. For them. He'd have to. For the good of his girls he'd do anything. After everything, they deserved a safe life—and more. He'd moved here for them. Left a high-paying job managing the elite Casa Bonita Restaurant in Los Angles for them.

No. That wasn't true, either.

He needed the move—the change of pace and the time together that life in a small town would afford—just as much as they did.

Maybe more.

If he squinted and didn't pay attention to the cracked drainpipes, the paint-chipped shutters, the overgrown trees with branches pressing against the home and the sixty-some-year-old original windows—sure, the place looked like a hidden fairy-tale house. The kind a secret princess might visit or run away to for safety. No wonder his daughters both stared at it in gap-mouthed wonder when he'd pulled up the drive. At ages five and three, they would see the cottage as a playhouse come to life.

The charm he'd imagined only a moment ago faded away upon entering.

His family couldn't live here. Not in its current condition. Doilies covered every inch of the front room. It smelled like mothballs and as if someone had spilled tea on the carpet countless times. A mauve color covered what he could see of the walls, but he couldn't see much of them for the amount of old belongings stacked so high. The kitchen was mustard yellow. *Everywhere.* Mustard-yellow appliances, counters, linoleum floor and painted walls. He tried to turn on the oven. It clicked, but the burner wouldn't start.

So it doesn't work, probably like 90 percent of everything in the house. Excellent.

He yanked at his hair.

Maybe the will hadn't been a way of God providing. What if it had been a test? What if he'd failed?

Kellen clenched his teeth. What made his aunt think the place would be a good home for a young family of three? It would take him a weekend just to childproof the place, let alone bring it up to code. Electricians and plumbers cost money. Ida had left him her savings—and there was a lot there. But without knowing what type of revenue the West Oaks Inn brought, he didn't want to start dipping into funds he might need to live on at some point.

"You have to lean your weight into the knob to get it to start."

The voice came from the doorway of the kitchen. He turned around and raised his eyebrows to the owner of it.

A woman with vivid, pale blue eyes stood there. Her eyes were the exact shade of the snow-fed streams high up in the Rockies where his parents used to take the family hiking every summer. A clear, pure color. She wore little or no makeup, something he could unfortunately spot after being around women in LA who painted beauty products all over their faces. Her skin had a healthy glow without the stuff. She looked—dare he say?—*real*. Her hair, on the other hand… She could have a lifelong career as the stand-in for the person who played Mufasa in *The Lion King* musical.

Kellen cleared his throat. "Excuse me?"

"To start the oven." She sidestepped him and leaned her hip against the oven while she twisted the knob. The burner ignited. "You just have to lean into it at the right angle. You'll get used to it."

He shook his head. "I won't have to."

"Oh." She laced her fingers together. "So you're not staying long term? I was hoping to meet my new neighbor."

"I'm kind of stuck here." He glanced out the window over the sink, which looked out onto the overgrown weed forest of a backyard. "Well—this is home for us, for now. If you catch my drift. And my first order of business will be tossing this oven—along with the rest of these old appliances." He ran his finger over the dust on the countertop. The whole room needed to be gutted.

She crossed her arms. "I take it you don't want to be here, then?"

Kellen scrubbed his hand down his face. "I'm here. That's what matters."

"That oven matters, too. To Ida."

He clicked the burner back off. "Ida's dead. I'm pulling this out tonight and putting it on the curb. So, no offense, but I won't ever need to learn how to lean just right."

She gasped. "You can't get rid of that oven." The woman touched the fridge as if feeling for a heartbeat. "Henry bought all these matching appliances for Ida to celebrate their one-year wedding anniversary. Ida cherished them and has taken the best care of them over the years. They were a gift of love."

Kellen had met Uncle Henry all of once. He knew Henry had been the mayor of Goose Harbor for quite some time before he died. But that was really all he knew about his father's oldest brother. The Ashby family had never been very close. Not with the age difference between the two brothers. Henry was sixteen years older than Kellen's dad. No wonder they hadn't kept in touch. Kellen's family was close with his mom's siblings growing up. Not the Ashbys.

"Well." He shrugged. "It's mine to get rid of, so…"

The woman shot him a glare.

His daughters pounded into the room.

Skylar—his little motormouth—ran right up to his knees and started tugging on his hand. "Outside there's a cat with kittens living by the bushes. Can we keep them? Please, Dad? Please?"

Kellen lightly turned both his daughters around to face the woman in the room. "These are my girls. Skylar." He placed his hand on her head. "And Ruthy." His quiet three-year-old buried her chin into her chest and clutched his hand.

Disregarding the kitchen floor that badly needed to be

mopped, the woman lowered herself to one knee to look the girls in the eye. "It's wonderful to meet both of you. There haven't been children living on this block in ages. You'll have so much fun in town."

"I don't think I caught your name," he said as he lifted Ruthy into his arms. Ruthy shoved her forehead against his shoulder.

"I'm Maggie. Maggie West." She offered her hand and he shook it with the wrong hand because his right arm held his daughter.

Ah. Now it all made sense.

This was the woman named in his aunt's will. What had the instructions said? That Kellen owned the inn but had to provide a place for Maggie West to live and let her continue working there.

He narrowed his eyes. Did she know she was protected in the will? The lawyer said that it would be up to Kellen to decide to tell her, but Ida might have told her when she drafted her legal paperwork. Or Maggie had suggested it to her. How much sway had the woman practiced over his aging aunt? Perhaps Maggie was a freeloader. Or had played on his aunt's emotions in order to be taken care of by a rich woman with no kids.

Women were good at hiding their motives. Experts at displaying fabricated emotions. Cynthia had taught him that lesson all too well.

Kellen would have to keep an eye on Maggie West—figure her out as best he could, since he was stuck providing for her at the moment.

All the people he'd run across in the past twelve years had been fueled by greed or want of fame. If it was fame Maggie was after… No, she didn't look as though she knew who he was. Maggie showed no signs of knowing that he'd once been a member of the rock band Snaggletooth Lions. So that—at least—was a small blessing.

He'd endured explaining to more than enough women that he signed away the rights to his royalties when he'd broken with the band. They all left the second they discovered he wasn't rich and had no plans to pursue fame ever again. Not that he'd been famous. Not really. The Snaggletooth Lions signed their record deal and made it big a month after he left the band. But people who looked up the Snaggletooth Lions online knew about his early involvement—that he'd written most of their songs that filled the radio air these days.

"I'm Kellen Ashby." He let go of her hand. "Ida's nephew."

Maggie tilted her head. "The one who's a dentist?"

So Ida had bragged about his brothers and not him. He worked his jaw back and forth and swallowed hard. Why leave him the house, then? Easy. She'd pitied him. Like the rest of his family.

Poor Kellen—the prodigal. Walked away from the church. Kids out of wedlock. The washed-up band member. His daughters spend most of their life in day care while he works eighty hours a week at the restaurant to pay their bills. Why couldn't he have turned out like his brothers? Like Bill or Tim or Craig?

He shook away his mother's words as they jumbled around in his head. "No. I'm afraid that's one of my far more successful older brothers. I have three to brag about if you want to hear their accolades sometime."

"I see. Maybe another time." Maggie took a step back. "Well. It was nice meeting all of you. I better get back over to the inn. You know where I am if you need anything or have questions about the house."

He pursed his lips. No help from the woman named in

Ida's will would be needed. "I think we can figure things out just fine on our own. But thank you for the offer."

She nodded, once, and left. Kellen watched her pick her way across the yard and enter the back door of the huge Victorian mansion next door.

"Can we keep the cats?" Ruthy finally spoke.

"You've always wanted a kitty, haven't you?" He brushed her strawberry blonde bangs to the side and kissed her forehead.

Skylar bounced up and down beside him. "Our old landlord said no—but you're the landlord now, Dad. Pleeeease."

The past five years had been full of him saying no to Skylar asking for something. Or telling her to be quiet or settle down so she didn't disturb the other people in the apartment complex they'd called home. He'd had to scold her so many times when she was just being a normal, excited kid. And shush her when she'd cried again and again, asking him why she didn't have a mom.

A knot he didn't realize was even there unwound from around his chest. For once he could say *yes* and let her enjoy a normal kid thing.

Holding tightly to Ruthy, Kellen got down on one knee. "No more landlords, sweetheart. This place is all ours. Go ahead and bring the kitties in, but keep them in your bedroom for now, okay? We'll see how many there are and pick one or two to keep and find homes for the others."

Ruthy couldn't get out of his arms fast enough. She trailed her sister as they bolted outside.

Kellen straightened up and looked back across the yard to study the mansion next door. The mansion he *owned*. The mansion his family should be living in right now. Ida's lawyer, Mr. Rowe, had shown him the inn's floor plans, and the private section was especially large. Four bedrooms and ample living space. Of course, he'd have to see it before he could decide what to do.

His girls deserved a big place to wander around in. Room to play on the floors and a place big enough for those ugly plastic play kitchens to fit and corners that could house a box stage for puppet shows. After being a father who was never around, he now wanted to give them the perfect home to put down roots in.

He just needed to get a better handle on Maggie before he could decide how to shove her out of the inn.

Chapter Two

❦

"I'm sorry to call you so early, but I don't know what to do." Maggie cradled the phone against her cheek as she peered out the kitchen window.

The Dumpster had arrived at eight in the morning. A Dumpster in Ida's front yard. Kellen's daughters buzzed around the cottage's backyard without any clue that their father was in the front yard destroying a chunk of their heritage. Why couldn't anyone understand that?

Watching Kellen pull Ida's belongings one by one onto the yard made Maggie's throat clam up. It felt as if someone had tied a heavy rock over her rib cage.

Paige, Maggie's closest friend in town, yawned on the other end of the phone call. "It's okay. I'm usually at school by now, but we're still on spring break."

"It isn't the weekend yet?" Maggie spun around to see her calendar fixed to the refrigerator with duct tape. It wasn't even on the right month anymore, and if it had been, she wouldn't have been able to see the date anyway because most of the calendar was covered by magnets holding up pictures, notes and recipes. Since she worked almost every weekend because that was mostly when guests came to the inn, she always seemed to have her days of the week wrong.

"Still just Friday." Paige's voice started to sound more normal now. Maggie definitely woke her up. "What's eating you, Mags? Bad guest? Is it that rude guy from Ohio again?"

Rude guy from Ohio? Mr. Boggs? He wasn't rude. Just a terrible flirt. He'd asked Maggie out on a date again the last time he was in town, but she'd said no. Mr. Boggs was nice enough in a bushy-mustache-and-balding sort of way, but he lacked the qualities on her list of things she wanted in a man. She'd fallen for a guy who didn't tick off everything on the list before. To make matters worse, Mr. Boggs was an art teacher—she'd dated the artist type once before, and that had ended terribly. Never again.

"Not that." Maggie surveyed the mess she'd made while fixing breakfast. Eggshell pieces littered the counter. Flour spilled onto the floor making it look as if a pack of raccoons had ransacked the place. Sugar trailed along the edge of the huge sink. Dirty plates and spatulas covered every other spare spot. The sweet scent of the morning's cinnamon rolls and maple sausage still lingered in the air. It mingled well with the sourdough bread turning gold in the oven.

Guests didn't go hungry while staying at the West Oaks Inn. Maggie made sure of that. She'd enjoyed her day off yesterday but sprung into action to make meals for today's guests.

The mess could be taken care of later. However, Kellen needed to be dealt with now. "Ida's nephew moved in next door."

"Is he cute?"

"Yes." She pressed the tips of her fingers over her mouth.

Why had that come out so quickly?

Maggie felt heat on her cheeks that had nothing to do with the bread baking in the oven. But what else could she say? Kellen Ashby had the type of blond, mussed hair that looked as if he rolled out of bed that way but probably took him an hour of styling to accomplish. His strong jaw brought ample attention to perfectly shaped lips. When he talked, she'd fought the desire to watch his lips move— there was an art in the way he spoke and a melodic tone to his voice that had made her want to linger in their conversation. He struck her as the type of guy who popped up the collar on his coat even when it wasn't cold out.

Basically not her type. At all.

He couldn't even play a convincing Prince Charming in a B-rated movie. Well, in the looks department he could— but as yesterday's ogre act about Ida's appliances showed, the personality similarities were nonexistent.

Paige growled on the other end of the line. "You can't just say *yes* and be done with it. Describe him."

"He has two little girls." She glanced around the curtain again. "I haven't spotted a woman yet, though, so I don't think there's a wife. But who knows? Maybe she's arriving later." Better to assume he had a significant other and be proven wrong. "So let's just say he's attractive and once again another taken man in Goose Harbor."

"Well, if you didn't call me to dish about the new guy and get dating advice, then what did you need?"

"I think he's getting rid of all of Ida's things." Maggie all but pressed her nose to the window to get a better look. Ida's prized oven was out on the lawn. After Maggie told him how important it was. Did the man have no heart?

"And that's a problem?"

"Paige, I don't think you get it." Maggie gripped the counter. "Those are Ida's things."

"Technically, if he inherited the house, then those are now his things."

"No. They're Ida's. They'll always be hers." Maggie picked up a small porcelain rooster that had belonged to her mother. The painted feathers caught sunlight as she twisted the figurine around and around. "Shouldn't he care about what was important to her?"

"Maybe you should ask him about it."

"I can't just walk over... Wait."

Kellen stalked down to the end of the driveway and stuck a garage-sale sign in the ground.

"Oh no. No. No."

"What, Maggie? You're starting to get me worked up. It's like talking to you as you watch a horror movie."

"You might as well be." It was one thing to think he was moving stuff outside to take stock or to part with a few of Ida's belongings. But it was a whole different matter if he planned to sell all of Ida's precious treasures. "I have to let you go. That man is about to get a piece of my mind."

"Hey, Mags—one thing."

Maggie patted her shirt, and a cloud of flour puffed into the air. "What?"

"Well, please say you won't be mad."

"Fine." She tucked her shirt in. No time to change. Besides, arguing with Kellen didn't require a wardrobe update. "Just tell me quick, because I need to get over there."

Paige took a deep breath. "I want you to keep in mind that Ida chose him—not you—to hand her belongings to. Remember that when you speak to him. Ida was a smart woman. I'm sure she had her reasons."

Paige didn't get it. How could she? Paige grew up in a wealthy family, still had both her parents and ended up married to an amazing man. Maggie would know. Paige's new husband, Caleb Beck, used to be Maggie's brother-in-law. Sure, Paige had experienced some hurt in life. But one broken engagement couldn't compare to losing a loved one to death. And Maggie had experienced the loss of four so far.

Ida had cared about those things Kellen was chucking into the Dumpster. So should he.

"Talk to you later." Maggie hung up.

Slipping on an old pair of loafers, Maggie flung open the back door and stormed into Ida's yard. Her heart pounded harder with every step. Kellen had set more of Ida's belongings in the yard than she'd been able to see from her vantage point in the inn. Side tables. Old frames with family pictures still inside. Mismatched teacups lined the edge of one table.

Maggie snatched up a cream-colored teacup with hand-painted leaves around the gold rim. They looked as if they were blowing in the wind—always in motion. The cup was beautiful. Ida had scoured countless resale shops and country fairs in order to find the best cups for her collection. She never settled for second-rate or mass-produced china.

Kellen appeared next to her elbow. "I haven't put prices on anything yet, so just make an offer on whatever you see that you like and let me know."

She spun around and was almost nose to nose with him. He had no right to smell so good. Against her better judgment she took a deep breath—fresh lemon with a slight mossy scent. Whatever cologne he wore she wanted to spritz it in her room before she climbed into her reading chair with a good book. It made her feel cozy in the same way she wanted to open her windows after a good rainstorm just to enjoy the air.

Who puts cologne on to work a garage sale?

An overmanicured man. That's who.

Exactly the type she didn't like to be around.

Maggie took a step back, making space. "How can you do this to Ida?"

He tilted his head. "I'm not doing anything to Ida. How can I?"

"By selling all of her stuff. You're hurting her memory." Maggie gestured to wave her hand over all the possessions scattered on the lawn. "You're basically saying you didn't care about Ida at all."

Kellen shrugged. "For starters, I didn't really know Ida. It's hard to care about someone you hardly knew."

"But that's just it. You *can* know her. See?" Maggie shoved the delicate china cup into his hand. "She loved drinking her daily tea from these mismatched cups. She had a different mug she used each day of the week and special ones for her friends. The one you're holding she used on Saturdays. It was precious to her. It should be to you, too."

He turned the cup around and around in his hand. "I guess it's interesting—if you can call a mug that." Kellen set it back in a box with the rest of Ida's china. "But I don't drink tea and it wouldn't hold enough coffee for my taste. My preference leans toward huge, ugly travel mugs. Anyway, I have no use for her china, so it can be sold."

Maggie picked the mug back up. "This cup has life because Ida loved it. Doesn't that mean anything to you?"

Kellen's face fell—as though he was suddenly disappointed or tired. "Things are just that—material possessions. That cup holds no more life than a mailbox. If I've learned one thing, it's that we should be more concerned with the time we have with the people we love than with objects that can be lost or broken or taken away at any minute. In the end, accumulating stuff doesn't matter. At least it shouldn't."

He couldn't understand. He'd never get it.

Maggie's arms trembled as she took a deep breath, easing the rage boiling right under her skin. Besides, who did he think he was—trying to teach her some sort of spiritual lesson? She knew better than anyone that time with people was the most important thing of all.

Maggie also knew that people left without warning, both in death and because they decided Goose Harbor wasn't exciting enough for them to stay. In the end, their belongings helped her remember them and she saw no harm in holding on to a few old possessions if they allowed her to recall a few good memories. Was that so bad?

Maggie pursed her lips. "Ida mattered. Why can't you see that? These things are your heritage. She chose to leave you her legacy and you're tossing it all away."

"No." He rested his hands on his waist and surveyed the lawn. "The money I'll make selling all of it—that is my heritage."

"So that's all you care about—the bottom line?"

Kellen laughed, once, in a clipped manner. The laugh held no humor. "I care so little about money…" He looked down the road and didn't speak for a moment. The muscle on the side of his jaw popped. "What I care about is providing a good life for my girls. That's what I'm doing." His vision landed back on her.

Maggie blinked back tears. "How much for the mug?"

"You can have it. No charge."

She had to get back to the inn before she started all-out crying. He'd already judged her for being materialistic. If she stayed any longer she'd start running her hands over everything that had belonged to Ida, remembering a story that went with each item. She'd turn into a blubbering mess and he'd think she had a screw loose. No one needed that.

Maggie nodded to him. Afraid to even thank him for letting her have the mug. On her way back home she made the mistake of walking past a table full of Ida's old books.

Maggie knew many of them were first editions and worth hundreds. Kellen probably didn't know and would give them away for a song. Maybe he deserved that. Then again, if he needed money to provide for his girls, she should tell him. She stared at the pile, biting her lip.

One book had fallen onto the dewy ground. Maggie bent to pick it up and then froze. She turned and stalked back to Kellen. "Her Bible?" Her voice rose. "You were going to sell her Bible? There is something seriously wrong with you."

Kellen's eyebrows formed a deep V. "Excuse me. I think you'd better—"

"If you cared about nothing in that house—" she stabbed her finger in the direction of the cottage "—if you sold every piece of it and bulldozed the entire property, you should have kept this. Out of everything, at least her Bible should have mattered." Maggie fanned the book open. Every available space on the pages was full of handwritten notes in Ida's shaky script. Each page was covered with pink, green and orange highlighter, and most of the text had been underlined at one point or another.

Maggie thrust the book into his hands. "These pages record a woman's faith journey. Do you see her notes in the margin? Every word in this book meant something to her. She held this Bible every day and it changed her life." Maggie no longer fought the tears as they fell down her cheeks. She snatched the Bible back, pressed it to her heart and crossed her arms over it. "You don't care about anything or anyone, do you, Kellen Ashby?"

He didn't even deserve to share Ida's last name.

Kellen worked his jaw back and forth. One of his girls giggled as they ran through the side yard together. He glanced at them and then back at Maggie. "I think you better leave."

"I'm keeping Ida's Bible. Someone who loved her should have it."

"Fine. Just go."

She turned her back to him but couldn't hold her tongue. "Are you going to tear down her house?" If he did, all of Ida would be gone. Forever.

"Not yet."

So he would someday. More than likely soon.

She clutched the Bible to her chest, splaying her palm against the grooves of the cross on the front cover. "But the cottage is beautiful. It has so much charm and fits in this town."

"Frankly I don't care about charm. I care about a house that fits the needs of my girls." His eyes trailed to take in the West Mansion behind her. "For now I'm going to gut the place and get rid of everything. I have a truck full of my things on its way here that I need to make room for."

"You're heartless." Where had that come from? Maggie never spoke like that. But this man, so far, brought out her worst.

He stalked forward, lowering his voice so his daughters, who were walking toward them, couldn't hear. "You can think whatever you want about me. But hear this. That house—" he jutted his thumb toward the cottage "—I own it. *Ida left it to me.* So you don't get a say in its future. For once in my life, no one is going to tell me how I should act or do things. Especially not a woman who has been freeloading off my aunt for who knows how long."

"Freeloading?" Maggie jerked her head back.

"I guess I forgot to tell you." He smirked. "Ida left me the inn, too."

Ice water filled her veins. She'd wondered…but hearing him say he owned her family home was much worse than she'd imagined.

When she didn't speak, Kellen continued. "So I'd be careful if I were you, Maggie. Because I have the right to sell the mansion, too."

Maggie spun back toward the inn and staggered through the yard. She fumbled with the latch on the gate that connected the two homes. At the moment she wished the three-foot-high picket fence was a ten-foot-tall cement wall so she couldn't see Kellen or the cottage. So she could block them out and pretend he didn't exist. But what did it matter?

He owned the West Oaks Inn.

Kellen Ashby could kick her out and tear down or sell the home she'd grown up in. The man who didn't care about the past owned her only connection to hers.

The legacy she'd lost.

Numb, Maggie opened the back door and strode past the mess in the kitchen.

She'd better start packing her things, because with the way she'd just spoken to her new boss, she could guarantee she was very soon to be homeless and unemployed.

"If you want to take in the sights, I can watch the girls for you." Mrs. Rowe—the lawyer's wife—smoothed her hand over the French braid she'd finished on Skylar's hair.

"Me next." Ruthy handed the older woman a hair tie and plopped down in front of her.

Kellen smiled as the three females laughed together. While his daughters loved when he gave them attention, they seemed to practically glow under the care of a woman. For the hundredth time he wished he could have given them a better mother in life. One day when he had to explain to them that their own mother hadn't wanted them, what would he say? That they meant so little to her that she'd signed away her rights the second Kellen offered to give up his claim to all the royalties he earned for writing the Snaggletooth Lions' popular songs?

He'd never pictured cozying up with Ida's lawyer and his wife, but he didn't know many people in town yet. Besides, they were a kind old couple who seemed taken with his daughters.

"We don't have any grandchildren of our own. Both of my sons decided to pursue careers instead of families. I'm afraid that's a thing with this generation." She tickled the back of Ruthy's neck, causing her to erupt with squeals.

He couldn't blame the Rowes' sons. Kellen had taken off from home with only his passion for music lodged in his heart. Not a dream of family. His daughters hadn't been planned. Family fell into his lap. But he'd choose them now. "Maybe your sons will change their minds."

Mr. Rowe ducked through the cottage's small doorway. "How'd the sale go today?"

"Not as well as I hoped, but then again, it's a Friday and people are working. I'll try again tomorrow. I really need to clear out the place before the truck with my stuff gets here."

"I could set you up for an auction. You might do better that way."

The lawyer was probably in his midfifties. Even though he wasn't working today, Mr. Rowe wore dress slacks with a tucked-in polo and shined dress shoes. Kellen doubted the man owned a single pair of jeans.

"That's a good idea."

"It'll take one call."

"Go ahead and do it." Kellen leaned his shoulder against the doorframe and watched his girls as they chatted with Mrs. Rowe. The woman pulled a baggie of cookies from her purse.

"Oh! Let's have a tea party." Skylar jumped up and

down and then proceeded to show Ruthy how to nibble her cookie "just-so." Because that was how ladies ate, apparently.

He'd have to dig back through the garage and save a few of Ida's unsold teacups for them. Maybe Maggie was right about keeping a few special belongings. His girls would imagine themselves queens of far-off lands if they were allowed to use Ida's china.

The lawyer pulled a smartphone from his back pocket. "You look stressed, son. Why don't you take a walk? It would do you good to have a breath of fresh air. My wife and I will stay with the girls."

Kellen really didn't want to leave Skylar and Ruthy with people he hardly knew. Then again, there was something he needed to take care of. "If you could stay with them for a couple minutes, actually that would be great."

He bowed out of the room and started toward the Victorian mansion next door. The sun had begun to set, making the sky purple, but even in the dim evening light the sage clapboard and pink-painted details on the home were easy to spot. The carved wood that trimmed every dormer and corner of the house spoke of a long-forgotten time period. Guests must bump down the driveway, gasping when they first saw the place, and look forward to the rest and relaxation they'd find inside.

The inn might belong to him, but the way he'd delivered the information to Maggie West had been nothing short of cruel. When she challenged him about redoing Ida's home, he'd spat out the word *freeloader* without thinking. She deserved an apology.

Maggie might be too attached to earthly treasures, but that was her beef to worry about, not his. It was just…he'd thought he'd escaped materialistic people by moving his girls away from Los Angeles. So much for his ideal vision of Goose Harbor being a safe haven to raise his family away from the worldly influences of the country's pop culture. He welcomed the realization, though—no place was perfect and he'd never be able to shelter his girls from everything. Not completely. At least people didn't walk around Goose Harbor half-dressed, although that could have more to do with the climate than anything else. Either way, that was one small victory.

Kellen eased through the gate that connected the two yards. He spotted Maggie right away. Knees in the wet dirt around the flower beds, Maggie yanked out weeds while mumbling under her breath. She worked quickly and had a smear of mud across her forehead. Kellen bit back a smile. The woman moved like the cartoon Tasmanian Devil. All frenzied motion. All passion.

Maybe that was why, despite wanting to steer clear of women who cared more about possessions than people, he felt drawn to her. When they'd argued earlier, a fire flicked across her eyes. Maggie West didn't do anything halfway. Even if something was going to be done wrong, it would be done with ten times more zeal than it required.

He stopped about a foot behind her. She yanked out a dandelion and tossed it over her shoulder.

The weed landed on his leather shoe. "Are you able to take a break?"

Hand to her heart, Maggie jumped. "I didn't hear anyone sneak up behind me." She stopped her laugh when she looked behind her and caught sight of him. "Oh. It's you."

"Listen. I want to talk to you. Can we sit on the steps for a minute?" He pointed toward the pink steps leading to the front door.

"Sorry. I can't stop." She kept her back to him. "I have so

much to get done and not enough hours to do it in. I really don't have time to talk to you right now."

"Please? It'll only take a few minutes."

She rocked back on her heels and squinted up at him. "Some people don't have the luxury of relaxing all the time. We have to work while other people get things handed to them. Besides, I wouldn't want anyone thinking I was freeloading, would I? Don't you want the flower beds of *your* inn to look good for the next guests arriving tomorrow?"

He chose to ignore the *freeloading* barb she'd tossed into the conversation, seeing as he'd come to apologize.

A story from the Bible played across his mind, as they'd been doing so often lately since he'd started reading it again. It was the part in the New Testament when Jesus spoke at Mary and Martha's house and Martha was too busy taking care of everyone to listen and became upset with Mary for sitting at the feet of Jesus instead of helping.

Did God want him to remind Maggie of that Bible story? It felt like it. But Kellen couldn't be sure. He'd spent so many years ignoring when he felt God wanted him to do something to know for certain. He might be a grown man, but despite being raised in the church, he was still only a young Christian.

With the way he had acted this morning, he couldn't blame her for being worried and upset after finding out he owned the place where she currently lived and worked— but he could end both of those emotions for her by being honest about the will.

He bent down to be eye level with her. "Martha, Martha. You are worried and upset about many things. Aren't you?"

Maggie turned back to the flower bed. "Not that it probably matters to you, but my name isn't Martha."

"I know."

She kept her eyes focused on the ground. "I'm surprised

that you know the Bible at all, seeing as you were going to ditch Ida's as quickly as an old newspaper."

Kellen forced his shoulders to relax as he held back the response that came to his lips. "My dad is a minister."

"Could have fooled me."

It was going to take everything in him to apologize to Maggie without snapping back at her. Kellen took a deep breath and counted to ten before speaking. "You're right. I wasn't a good church kid growing up. I rejected everything my dad taught and lived life by my terms for a long time. God kept chasing me, though, and I'm His for good now. The funniest thing is, now my dad's old sermons keep coming back to me at the oddest times."

She yanked out another weed.

He moved a foot away and kneeled in the flower bed.

She watched him out of the corner of her eye. "You'll ruin those fancy designer jeans."

Kellen ran his fingers over the mulch. "I always wondered if Martha had just asked the people gathered to hear Jesus talk if they would help her, the chores could have all been done in a couple minutes and then she could have been sitting there at the Lord's feet next to her sister."

"Maybe she had no one to ask. Or maybe she knew it would be a waste of time to ask because no one would come to her rescue. Maybe Martha was all on her own and knew her sister wasn't about to leave what she was doing to help." She yanked out a weed with so much force it took out the flower next to it, as well. "Maybe, like me, she had no choice. What if she felt like she was drowning and losing what she cared about and she…?" Maggie shook her head. "So don't talk to me about helping."

Dare he challenge her? "Is it that you're alone, or is it that you refuse to ask for help?"

"You don't understand what I'm saying." She shot him

a glare and inched farther away. "I'm done talking to you."

Kellen yanked out a weed.

Maggie rocked back onto her heels and let out a huff. "Just what are you doing?"

He shrugged. "Sharing the load."

"I'd rather not be around you right now. I know this inn belongs to you and I'll leave as soon as you say so, but for now I just want an evening to remember how beautiful it is and—"

Kellen sat down firmly and faced her. "Maggie, you need to chill for a second. I came here to tell you that I'm not going to— Ouch." A small stabbing pain shot into the side of his neck. Then another. He swatted his neck, and his hand collided with a large bug. Another one buzzed near his ear. "Bees."

No. Not again.

Maggie got to her feet. "Did they sting you?"

His throat was already closing up. A rush of blurry warmth flooded his brain. "Allergic." He wheezed out the word. Why did it have to be his neck? Swelling there would make his breathing much harder than his normal reaction. The bees had chosen to inject their poison in the worst place possible.

Black dots painted across his vision. Kellen tried to stand, but he fell backward.

Maggie wrapped her arm around his shoulders and helped him stumble to a lounge chair.

"Do you only get a rash, or are you allergic-allergic? Is this a CPR type of thing? Because I took training once, but I'm not real confident. Do I need to call for an ambulance?" Her eyes were wide, searching his face.

Kellen fought to keep his eyes open, but the whole world

was swirling. Maggie's hair looked twice as big as normal. "EpiPen. My bathroom. Black bag. Quick."

The last thing he saw was Maggie taking off across the yard.

If he died, what would happen to his girls?

Chapter Three

Shoving open the front door to the cottage, Maggie banged into a couch that had been moved to a new location. Ida used to have all the furniture lining the walls. But this wasn't Ida's home any longer, was it?

Maggie's body shook with adrenaline as she sucked in a ragged breath.

Four sets of eyes landed on her. All of them held questions.

Mr. Rowe grabbed her arm to steady her. "Maggie. You don't look so well."

"Emergency. It's medical. Call 9-1-1."

"What's wrong, dear?" Diane, Mr. Rowe's wife, wrapped her arms around the two little girls.

Maggie's thoughts piled up together like an accident on the expressway. How much information should she tell them? No time. She needed to help Kellen.

The bathroom. She had to find the black bag.

Used to stressful situations as a lawyer, Mr. Rowe already had his cell phone to his ear. "Yes. We need an ambulance. Someone is hurt." He rattled off the address to the cottage as he walked out the front door.

Maggie pointed at Skylar. "Do you know where your dad keeps his EpiPen?"

Skylar gave one brave nod before taking off. She returned a second later and handed the injector to Maggie. "A bee sting?" Her voice wavered.

Maggie wanted to stop and hug her, but she knew Kellen needed the shot. And although she wasn't well versed when it came to allergic reactions, she also knew time mattered. She prayed that Mrs. Rowe would be able to comfort the girls.

"My dad is hurt?" Ruthy dissolved into tears. "Is he gonna die?"

"I want to go with you." Skylar trailed Maggie to the door. Her little hands fisted at her sides.

Maggie wasn't about to let the little girl see her dad wheezing and in pain. Not at such a young age. If only someone had protected her from the pain of learning about her own father's death all those years ago. And more recently, of seeing her mother suffering from illness for so long. Maggie shook those thoughts away.

Action. Right now she needed to stop thinking and act.

Grabbing Skylar's shoulders, Maggie squeezed them once. "Your dad needs you to go back inside and pray for him. That's the best thing you can do for him right now. Can you do that? Mrs. Rowe will help you, okay? I need to go give this to him." She waved the EpiPen.

Without waiting to see if Skylar had obeyed, Maggie sprinted back across the lawn. Thankfully Mr. Rowe had left the gate propped open so she wouldn't have to worry about messing with the rusted latch.

The lawyer was still on the phone with 9-1-1 when she got back to Kellen. Being a blond, Kellen had a pale complexion to begin with, but his skin looked sickly and ashen. His head was tipped to the side.

Maggie tapped his shoulders. "Can you hear me? Kellen. Please. I don't know what I'm doing."

Unresponsive.

Mr. Rowe covered the mouthpiece to the cell phone. "Open up the pen. Hold it to his thigh and press the trigger. Count to ten and then massage the area for ten seconds, as well." He turned back to his phone. "Yes. I'm still here. The victim has lost consciousness. I'll be at the end of the drive to flag them to the right location. I initially gave the address to the next-door neighbor's house."

He took off toward the street.

Please, God. Calm my nerves. Let Kellen be all right.

Following Mr. Rowe's instructions, she removed the cap and held the end to Kellen's thigh. Hopefully the shot was strong enough to work through his jeans.

She took a deep breath and pressed the button.

"One. Two. Three. Four." She licked her lips and looked back at Kellen's face. *Be okay. Please be okay.* His daughters needed their daddy. They shouldn't have to grow up having lost their dad in a tragic accident as Maggie had lost hers. No little girl should experience that pain. "Five. Six. Seven. Eight. Nine. Ten."

She put the cap back on, covering the shiny needle that now showed, and then tucked it under the lounge chair. Maggie watched Kellen's face, hoping to see an instant change. She put her hand where she'd used the EpiPen and massaged the area as Mr. Rowe had instructed her to.

Seeing no immediate change in Kellen's condition, she took the advice that she'd told Skylar only a minute ago. Pray. That was the best way to help him.

"Please, Lord, save him. Let him recover without any lingering problems."

All the stress from the past few minutes rushed over her, making her blink back tears. She shouldn't have argued with him…again. If she'd gone to the porch and talked as he had asked, they wouldn't have been near the bees. Sure, he might have been about to tell her to skedaddle, but being kicked out wouldn't be as bad as letting him get hurt. If she wouldn't have been so stubborn—like always—none of this would have happened.

"Don't let anything bad happen to Kellen."

Kellen shifted on the chair. Maggie looked back at his face to see him watching her through a half-lidded gaze. Never in her life had she been so happy to see a man's blue eyes. She leaned forward and grabbed his hand. "You're okay? Thank You, God."

He put his free hand over his swollen neck. Letting her know he couldn't speak yet. He squeezed the hand she held twice. She imagined that meant *thank you*.

A cool spring breeze swept over them, and Kellen shivered. From the cold, from shock or the medication coursing through his body, she didn't know.

"I'll go get a blanket." She started to get up.

But Kellen tightened his hold of her hand and shook his head.

Maggie sat down on an open area of the lounge chair and stared at the flower beds surrounding the West Oaks Inn. Usually the sight of the happy flowers bobbing in the wind made her smile. But at the moment she wanted to pull them all up by the roots. Keep the bees away from Kellen for good. She'd have to warn him about the local beekeeper who lived a few blocks away. Kellen should avoid that part of town. And start carrying his EpiPen.

He shivered again, so Maggie cupped his hand in both of hers, hoping that comforted him.

Reflections from the emergency lights on the ambulance bounced off the mansion's windows. A team of EMTs raced forward with a stretcher. Maggie caught sight of the dark-haired Joel Palermo, the newest member of the Goose Harbor Fire Department, as he strode toward them purposefully.

While the other men lifted Kellen onto the stretcher, Joel turned his attention toward Maggie. "Can you run through what happened?"

She gave him a play-by-play of the bee sting and estimated how many minutes between the stings and the EpiPen injection. "I hope I did it right."

Joel smiled. "You must have, since he came to. Great work, Mags. We'll take it from here, but this man has you to thank for saving his life."

And for putting it at risk.

He shouldn't have been weeding. By flowers. In spring. When bees were always out.

The EMTs maneuvered the stretcher into the ambulance.

Joel reached out to help Maggie climb into the back. "Are you coming with us?"

Suddenly very self-conscious, Maggie bit her lip. "Perhaps there's someone closer to him who should go."

Mr. Rowe pressed his hand into the small of Maggie's back and propelled her forward. "Kellen doesn't have a wife. It's just him and the girls. Me and Diane will watch Skylar and Ruthy for as long as he needs. You go on with Kellen to the hospital. Call me when you need to be picked up." He ushered her right to Joel's outstretched arm.

Before Maggie could decide if accompanying Kellen was a good idea or not, the men in the ambulance closed the back door and turned on the sirens.

Joel pointed to a metal ledge near the stretcher. "Go ahead and have a seat. Hold his hand for me. It helps calm them down."

Maggie grabbed hold of Kellen's hand again. She looked

back up at his face. Through the oxygen mask he offered her a small smile before closing his eyes again.

Maggie glanced through the blinds on the kitchen window for the tenth time, trying to see if Kellen had made it back home.

Her inn guests had raved about breakfast, but after getting back to the inn at one in the morning, she lacked the energy she usually saved for visiting with the tourists. They'd borrowed some of the bicycles she kept stocked in the garage and had headed into town for the day.

The mess in the kitchen was bigger than normal, but it could wait until later. Intent on taking a nap, she made her way back to her bedroom. Maggie dropped onto the bed and flung her hand to the side. It hit a lump under the cover. She moved back the sheets. Ida's Bible. She trailed her fingers over the soft, worn leather cover.

Honestly a nap wasn't going to happen. Every time she attempted to take one, it never came to fruition. She'd just lie there and think of fifty things she could be spending her time accomplishing. Relaxing always made her feel guilty—as if she should be doing something better with her time. If she did fall asleep, she always woke up grumpy. Those scientists who touted the benefits of a midday nap missed interviewing her.

Gathering the Bible under her arm, Maggie headed out to the back porch. As doubts and fears swirled in her heart, she would have loved speaking with Ida today, but reading the old woman's notes in the margin of her Bible would be just as good.

Besides, Maggie probably needed to read scripture more than she needed to talk to her friend. It had been a while since she cracked the spine on her Bible. The problem was, more often than not anymore, doing so proved pointless.

God's promises weren't for her. If they had been, her life would have been different.

She opened the cover and realized she had the book upside down. About to flip it back around, Maggie stopped when she saw a list of names. Hers was there, and scribbled next to it with an addition sign was Kellen's. The top of the list read Pray For Daily.

Maggie dabbed her eyes. She'd known that Ida loved her but hadn't known the woman had devoted time to praying for her every day. Had Maggie ever done that for another person? Sadly the answer was no.

She ran her finger down the list. Names had been added to the bottom later in a different ink—including Maggie's friend Paige. Maggie pressed her fingers over her smile, remembering Paige's first few days in Goose Harbor and how Ida had literally latched on to the new schoolteacher. Ida always said she knew when someone was ready to fall in love, and that had proved true with Paige and Caleb. Ida all but shoved those two together and now they were happily married.

Too bad Ida never found a Prince Charming type for Maggie. If only.

Maggie went back to her name. Odd how it shared a number with Kellen when there had definitely been more room to add one of their names to its own line. Next to their names Ida had scribbled two verses. Zechariah 1:3 and Romans 5:5. Beside the Romans reference in tiny letters it said: *I will never stop hoping.*

Maggie found the table of contents to see what page in the Bible the book of Zechariah started on. She flipped to it and read Zechariah 1:3—*Therefore tell the people: This is what the Lord Almighty says: "Return to me," declares the Lord Almighty, "and I will return to you," says the Lord Almighty.*

Was it possible that Ida worried that Maggie had fallen away from her faith in the Lord? The passage made Maggie feel that way. *Had* Maggie turned from God? Maybe a little. Was it possible to do something like that "only a little"? It seemed like an all-or-nothing sort of thing.

Maggie let her gaze lift up and rest on the small river that ran behind the West Oaks Inn and continued on past Kellen's property. The backyard neighbor had a small working water mill that slapped against the water day and night. The sound always comforted Maggie—it was constant, but somehow she tuned it out most of the time. Or had just grown used to it.

Had God become like that mill in her life? There, but ignored? Was He making noise—trying to get her attention day in and day out with her ignoring Him? She'd never considered that. Sure, she was still frustrated about her lot in life. In her thirties without much to her name, no prospect of marriage, no family and about to lose the only home she'd ever known—the legacy of the West family.

Who wouldn't feel defeated and abandoned after that?

But, as usual, her situation didn't change the truth. God was God, and He got to decide if she lived a good life or not. She had to find her grit and keep moving forward. As she always did. Maybe He would have been easier on her if her heart wasn't so prone to wandering and she wasn't always getting distracted. There had to be something she was doing wrong. If not, her life would be different—He'd be blessing her, right? That was what they always said in church.

"God. Forgive me," Maggie whispered. "I didn't realize it, but I have been closed off to You. If I'm being honest, I've been mad that You've taken so many people that I loved from this earth. But maybe I should think of it as You had surrounded me with so many wonderful people—

people You wanted to graduate to heaven quickly because they all loved You so much."

A peace washed through her. Something she couldn't quite explain. It was like drinking ice water on a one-hundred-degree day. Maggie closed her eyes for a moment, enjoying the feeling before opening them again and flipping to the book of Romans in the Bible.

She found Romans 5:5 right away—*And hope does not put us to shame, because God's love has been poured out into our hearts through the Holy Spirit, who has been given to us.*

Ida had written that she would never stop hoping. It clearly applied to both her and Kellen. Hoping that they'd return to the Lord? Hoping they'd realize God loved them? That Ida loved them?

Maggie would never know.

Ida was gone and she couldn't ask her. But she knew one thing—Ida loved her and Ida loved Kellen. A woman didn't put the name of someone on a list in her Bible and choose to pray for them daily unless she loved that person. If Maggie wanted to protect the belongings that were special to Ida, how much more important must Kellen be to the woman Maggie had looked up to? If the teacups mattered, Kellen mattered even more.

"Miss Maggie?" A small voice interrupted her thoughts.

Skylar and Ruthy stood at the bottom of her steps with Mrs. Rowe not far behind.

Maggie closed the Bible and set it on the bench next to her. "Hi, girls. To what do I owe the pleasure of seeing your beautiful faces?"

Mrs. Rowe nodded to them.

Skylar took Ruthy's hand and helped her up the steps. Ruthy shoved a bouquet of wildflowers and dandelions toward Maggie.

Skylar smiled. "We came to thank you for saving Daddy's life."

Ruthy nodded solemnly. "I love him."

Maggie leaned forward and accepted the flowers. "I'm glad I could help. How's your dad doing?"

Ruthy finally offered a smile as she whispered, "He's singing."

Skylar patted Maggie's knee. "That means he's really good. Daddy likes to sing. It's his favorite thing in the world."

"I'm so glad to hear that. Do you girls want to come inside and help me find a vase?"

Skylar was at the door before Maggie got up from her seat. "You always smell like cinnamon."

"Thanks." Maggie grimaced at Mrs. Rowe. "I think."

Mrs. Rowe yawned. She wore the same outfit she had on yesterday, meaning she had yet to be back home since the bee-sting incident and probably needed a break.

Maggie offered her hand to Ruthy, who shyly took it. "Diane, you can head home. Let Kellen know I have the girls entertained here and he can give a call whenever he feels up to having them come back home. They're welcome here all day if he'd like to rest. Let him know that, okay?"

Diane Rowe mouthed *Thank you* and headed back toward the cottage.

Maggie continued into the kitchen and helped both the girls into aprons, folding the fabric over and tying the waist part under their armpits just like the way her mother used to do with her. "Who wants to help me make some brownies?"

"I do!"

"Me!"

"Know what, Miss Maggie?"

Maggie smiled down at Skylar, smoothing her hand over the girl's hair. "What, sweetheart?"

"We picked the kittens we're going to keep. A black one and an orange one."

"The black one had white paws!" Ruthy chimed in.

Skylar nodded. "We're naming them Pete and Repeat. Isn't that silly?"

Maggie laughed along with them and promised to visit the kitties soon. "Now, let's have some fun." Maggie handed out spoons and cranked the volume on the local Christian radio station to high. Both girls started singing along. Their smiles were infectious.

If Maggie was going to get kicked out of the inn by their father anyway, she could still make a few fun memories with the two sweet little girls. Her eviction wasn't their fault. All they knew was that their daddy could have died last night. Maggie would do whatever she could to erase the memory of their fear. Brownies were a good start.

Kellen winced on the way over to the inn.

He'd forgotten how sore an EpiPen shot could make his leg. The bruise it left was nothing short of impressive. Besides the soreness, he felt fine, though, so he needed to continue with getting things in order before Skylar started school on Monday. Mrs. Rowe had offered to watch Ruthy during the workday for the next month until he was settled and could decide if she'd stay around the inn with Kellen during the day or if he'd sign her up for formal day care.

First on the list, he needed to assess the business at the West Oaks Inn. Kellen didn't want to. Not after Maggie had been so great last night. She'd stayed with him at the hospital. Refilled his water jug whenever it got down to the halfway mark and gone on a mission to find him trail mix from a vending machine located on a different level of the hospital. She'd seemed to thrive off of taking care of someone.

Or she was doing her best to get on his good side now that she knew he owned the mansion.

He almost wished he hadn't told her. It would have been useful to study her a little longer and be able to decide if she was out to get something from his aunt or if she was what she appeared to be—a caring and passionate person who enjoyed serving others.

Kellen would probably never get to know the honest answer now. What did it matter? His track record at assessing people's characters wasn't all that great to begin with. Why start trying now?

He couldn't put off seeing the ledgers and making choices concerning the inn any longer. He had to plan the best moves to provide for his family. If the inn was working in an efficient manner as he hoped, he could leave it be.

If her reaction to him gutting Ida's home was any indication, change and Maggie didn't go well together. He hoped the bed-and-breakfast worked like a well-oiled machine. If not, he'd have to make some changes whether or not Maggie West approved.

Back when his friend had offered him the restaurant-manager position at Casa Bonita as a favor, Kellen didn't know how he would handle the pressure of such a different job. Lead guitar and singer of a rock band versus managing a five-star restaurant—talk about different worlds. But then, it hadn't been such a stretch in retrospect. Long hours. Late nights. Lots of time on his feet.

During the Snaggletooth Lions' early days, Kellen had been the one to schedule their tours, meet with marketing professionals and interview agents. Managing was already like second nature to him by the time he left the band. Good thing his friend had believed in him enough to hand over Casa Bonita. How would he have provided for his daughters if that job hadn't fallen into his lap?

Kellen ran his hand through his hair.

God had provided. All along, even when Kellen wasn't being faithful—God was there. Just as He was now. God had worked through Ida to provide a new life for his girls and him. A way out of the busy existence that had become the norm in LA. In Goose Harbor he'd have more time with the girls. He didn't want them to be in day care eleven hours a day ever again.

As he neared, music filtered out the open kitchen windows with his girls' laughter sprinkled in for good measure.

He tapped on the back door and waited for an answer. They couldn't hear him. Kellen cracked open the door and couldn't help the grin on his face.

Maggie, Skylar and Ruthy danced around the kitchen singing into spatulas. The kitchen looked as though a cookie factory had exploded inside it—mid mixing. Flour painted every surface, and chocolate chips littered the large island counter.

He loved seeing his daughters having a good time, but who paid for the flour and sugar and eggs that had been spilled everywhere? Perhaps he was mean-hearted to think about the bottom line, as Maggie had alluded to the other day. But was the waste Maggie's goods or was she used to Ida footing the bill on everything and didn't care what got spilled?

"Daddy!" Skylar spotted him first.

Maggie blushed profusely and set down her spatula. "I said just to call when you were ready for them."

"I don't have your number." He hollered over the music. Kellen eyed the radio.

Maggie read his mind and turned the music down. "The

number to the inn is on the internet. You could have looked it up."

"I came to see the office."

Skylar flashed a toothy grin. "We're making brownies, Daddy. From scratch."

"I can see that." He cupped her head and dropped a kiss on her hair as he walked past.

Maggie twisted a dishrag in her hands. "The office for the inn?"

"That's the only one I think is here."

"It's a mess." She wiped the countertop with the rag but only succeeded in spreading the flour.

Kellen raised his eyebrows. "That sort of thing seems to be going around."

She moved to block the hallway. "Why don't you let me clean the office first? Come back next week."

"The inn is my responsibility now." Clearly the office was down the hallway. Kellen eased closer. "I'd rather have a look-see and get started on coming up with the best plan of action for moving forward."

Her eyes grew wide. "Plan of action?"

"Just point me in the right direction."

"Okay." She pointed to the right. "It's through the hall. Second door on the left. Don't say I didn't warn you."

Kellen stopped to hug both of his girls before heading to the office. The wooden floor creaked with every step. Was the whole house like that? Guests wouldn't enjoy or return to a place with floors that creaked like mad. He'd have to walk the whole place with a pad of paper and a pen and document everything that needed to be updated.

He opened the door to the office, and his mouth dropped open.

Paper stacked a foot tall covered the floor except for a small walkway that led to the desk. And what was the point of a desk if he couldn't even see the surface of it? Kellen entered the room and turned in a slow circle. If this signaled how Maggie kept—or didn't keep—records, the inn was in worse shape than he'd thought.

He laced his fingers together around the back of his neck.

He'd manage. Didn't he always? Casa Bonita had been a wreck, too, when his buddy hired Kellen to manage the restaurant. He knew nothing about the restaurant business when he started that job, and now Casa Bonita had one of the best revenue streams in the greater LA area.

Kellen would figure out the bed-and-breakfast industry, too.

Maggie peeked into the room. "I got the girls settled down in my living room with fresh brownies and a Disney movie. I hope that's okay."

"It's fine. Thanks for taking care of them this morning. It sounded like they were having a lot of fun."

"Anytime. Seriously. They're a blast to have around."

"On that note." Kellen took two steps toward her, which in the small room brought them within a stride of each other. "I wanted to thank you for saving my life last night."

Maggie toed the floor. "You wouldn't have been stung if I had gone and talked to you like you asked."

"Who knows? The past isn't worth worrying about or reliving. I say, keep moving forward without thinking about the *could haves* or *should haves*. You know?"

"Some of the past is worth reliving."

And that was really the crux that divided Kellen and Maggie. She wanted to stay connected to the past. So much that, for what he'd seen of the inn so far, she filled every nook and cranny with half-broken antique junk. Whereas Kellen wanted to leave the past as it was. Reliving his past meant seeing every mistake he'd made over and over again. No, thanks. He'd rather focus on the future. On who he could become instead of the man he once was.

Keep moving forward.

"Yes." He pressed his palms together and touched the tips of his fingers to his chin. "Take, for example, when you decided to start piling up all these documents—why don't we relive that moment right now?"

"Are you going to get rid of me?" Her voice dropped so low he had to lean forward to hear her.

"No." He answered honestly but decided to leave out the fact that even if he wanted to he couldn't fire her. "But I am about to change every single aspect of this inn. I hope you're ready for that."

The fire blazing in her eyes said she'd never be ready.

Too bad.

Chapter Four

Maggie rooted through her dresser for a pair of jeans that weren't completely worn out or stained from one too many cooking accidents. But finding something nice to wear had suddenly become the most difficult task in the world. How long had it been since she bought new clothes?

She ran her fingers down the sleeve of a sweater hanging in her closet. The hole in the elbow had been there when the garment belonged to her mother. Bunching the fabric, she rubbed it on her cheek. Soft. Comforting. Sensible. What clothes should be. What her entire wardrobe consisted of. Her clothes suited her, or at least had always seemed to.

Until now.

Today everything screamed rumpled, overlooked and dull. Had she really been walking around looking like that for the past ten or more years? How depressing. What must the people in town think? Probably the truth. *There goes Maggie, all alone. So sad.*

Not that it mattered. Clothes and looks shouldn't—didn't—matter. Right?

She let out a huff of hot air. Surely her friends Paige or Shelby could have told her. Someone who cared should have staged an intervention. But perhaps no one cared—not really. *Not enough.* Maggie always found herself in the position of rescuing, comforting and encouraging. Very rarely did her friendships go the other way around. She'd never thought about that until now.

Maggie fisted her hands.

The floorboard on the top stair of the grand staircase in the lobby creaked. Even from her bedroom in the private portion of the inn, she could hear it. It creaked again. And again. Kellen must be rocking back and forth on the step—trying to figure out how much replacing and refinishing the wood was going to cost him.

Just like every day in the past week, he'd been holed up in the inn's office already when she got up to make breakfast for the guests. Then today after the last elderly couple checked out and the inn was empty, he'd set off with a ruler, a pad of paper and his phone. Said he had to assess the place. Whatever that meant.

After yanking a pair of dark-wash jeans from the bottom of the stack, she shook them out—they were so stiff from rarely being put on.

Sarah, her younger sister, had purchased the dressier jeans as a present for Maggie's birthday almost three years ago. At the time, Maggie had told her sister that she was going to return them, but she hadn't been able to do so after losing Sarah soon after that.

Maggie slipped them on and found a lightweight shirt without too many wrinkles to go on top—it was a shirt she normally saved for greeting new guests at check-in. But Maggie needed to look respectable—if only to give her the confidence boost she needed to ask Kellen for money. Anything to help her case.

On her way out the door she peeked in her mirror, adjusting the clip in her hair after she smoothed down wayward strands. With a deep breath, she stepped into the hallway. As she walked, she traced her fingers along the wall. The feel of the slight embossing of the wallpaper breathed strength into her veins. This was her home. She'd been born here. Took her first steps as a child in the grand entrance. Used to race her sister down the stairs by sliding on the banister. The mansion that made the West Oaks Inn had been in her family's possession since the founding of Goose Harbor, and while it had been changed when it was first converted into an inn, most of the original character had been saved.

Well—not possession. Maggie had lost the title of owner five years ago. When she'd run out of funds. When her mother passed away, she'd left everything to both Maggie and Sarah, but after Sarah married Caleb she'd chosen to hand over everything to Maggie. Sarah said she and Caleb had enough to manage with starting a nonprofit; they couldn't afford to help pay for the mansion's expenses, as well. That left Maggie to pay all the bills, but her job as a cook at a local diner hadn't brought in enough income. Expenses on the mansion ate into the savings like ants in a picnic basket. And the savings hadn't amounted to the great West fortune that they were known for. Not after using it to pay for so many medical expenses for her grandmother and mother toward the end. Experimental treatments weren't covered by insurance.

Thankfully Ida had offered to purchase the house and let the rest of town believe that Maggie still owned it. Converting the old home into a bed-and-breakfast had been Ida's idea, as well. *Think, Magpie. Just think. A ready income right from the mansion.* Ida and her husband had possessed the ability to see possibilities and hope when no one else did. Whether it be in relation to business, government or matters of the heart.

Prior experience told Maggie that the ache in her chest would last for the rest of her life. Ida hadn't been a blood relation, but she had been as close as family. And now she was gone. Just like everyone else important to her. At least now there was no one left to lose.

Maggie checked the pink envelope in the drawer by the oven one last time. Empty. Ida had always left cash in there—money for Maggie to buy food for the breakfasts and goodies she prepared for guests or cleaning supplies or new items for the inn. Of course, Kellen wouldn't know about the system. But with all the prowling through stacks of paperwork in the office he'd engaged in yesterday, she figured he'd bring up money at some point. With a fridge going bare it was now up to her to broach the subject. How embarrassing.

In the past few years, why hadn't she planned and saved for the possibility that Ida wouldn't leave the inn to her? She'd just assumed everything would work out. But hoping for the best had gotten her into most of her scrapes in life, hadn't it? Sure, she'd tried to act as she'd been taught— to be a good Christian, do everything the right way and trust that God would take care of her. But what had that gotten her? Nothing.

Most of the private section of the inn had stayed true to the original structure of the mansion. Ida had made a point of that for Maggie's sake. She'd also insisted that the private part of the inn be large enough to house a family, although Maggie had told her that wasn't needed. An old sitting room had been divided and converted into two bedrooms, and rooms that had belonged to servants long before Maggie was born now served as her bedroom and the office. The original mansion had a large footprint that led to the private portion remaining big. Wallpaper chosen by her grandmother covered the walls—bare in some

spots—but each inch held memories. Her great-aunt leaning against the kitchen counter near the window. Grandpa
telling stories as Maggie and her sister played on the large
Oriental rug in the living room.

As she pressed through the door that led to the public
portion of the inn, a little bell attached to the hinge tin-
kled. The furniture in the entryway needed a good dusting. She should probably give the welcoming room a good
floor scrub, too.

Stop stalling.

Kellen stood at the top of the stairs with the end of the
pen between his teeth, his eyes glued to his pad of paper.
Just like the other times she'd seen him, he was dressed
nicer than people in Goose Harbor normally were. Sure,
he had jeans on, but they looked as though they'd been
made for him—and only him—to wear. Were tailor-made
jeans even a thing? The untucked black button-down shirt
he wore had a sheen to it, and he looked as if he'd spent a
good twenty minutes styling his blond hair into perfectly
disheveled spikes.

"Kellen?" She rested her hand on the intricately carved
knob on the banister.

His head snapped up. "You scared me. I didn't hear
you come in."

"Can you spare a minute?"

"Sure. Come on up here." He motioned with his hand
for her to join him.

Nerves skittered around inside Maggie's stomach as
she climbed the stairs. Kellen kept his eyes on her, a slow
smile spreading across his face as she made her way to the
landing. He probably wouldn't greet her cheerfully if he
knew she was coming to ask—no, beg—for some money.

When she reached the top he handed her his pad of

paper. "I didn't realize how many things need fixing. It's overwhelming."

Why was she anxious? She was Maggie West. A member of one of the founding families. The person people turned to when they needed anything in town. She usually had a quip to throw back at someone and prided herself on speaking her mind. Maybe that would all start when she felt more comfortable with Kellen. But probably not. He was her boss, after all. He had the power to demolish her beloved family home if he really wanted to.

She had no power. No control. And never would. Not where her home was concerned. Not in her life. She braced a hand on the wall as the realization rocked through her.

If only she hadn't trusted Alan. If she still had her money she could...what? Make an offer on the inn? It was unlikely that Kellen would have sold even if she hadn't lost everything.

Instead of glancing at the list, she looked him right in the eye. "The house is just fine."

"From the outside, sure, don't get me wrong, it's gorgeous. But things aren't always what they seem. Believe me. In the deep and hidden places, this house needs work." He held out his hand.

Maggie moved to give him back his list, but he latched on to her hand instead and led her down the hallway.

"Like this." He let go of her hand when they stopped in front of one of the large, rounded sitting windows that flagged each end of the upstairs hallway. Maggie had spent many happy hours of her youth tucked in the widow alcove, sitting on the cushion with her face pressed to the glass—dreaming of a future that never materialized.

Kellen tugged the cushion away and moved the curtain to the side. He pressed down on the windowsills and the wood that made up the bench seat. "See that? It's soft. Wood rot."

Did he think she hadn't taken care of the place? She'd always done the best she could. "But—"

"Here, let me show you some more stuff."

He replaced the cushion and stood. Taking a step behind Maggie, Kellen laid his hand on the small of her back to steer her to walk with him. Wow. The man smelled good. It wasn't the normal woodsy smell that most men Maggie had known chose to wear. Kellen's cologne—or shampoo, whatever it was he used—carried an almost citrusy freshness. It reminded Maggie of her many trips to the Crest Orchards that lay on the edge of town.

Between getting over to the inn before seven in the morning, preparing Skylar for school and dropping Ruthy off with the Rowes, when had he found time to shower?

"Kellen." She knew he was close behind her but didn't realize he was literally right on her heels, and when she stopped in her tracks he knocked into her. Her balance compromised, she ended up with her back against the wooden paneling and Kellen's hands braced on either side of her.

How had they ended up so close? She scanned his face quickly before meeting his eyes again. A light stubble marched across his jawline. She hadn't noticed that the other times she'd seen him. He always looked freshly shaven. Had he been too rushed today? Or forgotten? Maybe, just maybe, Kellen Ashby didn't have his world quite as put together as he appeared to.

Kellen hovered a few inches away from her. "I have a couple questions for you."

Why was he still standing so close to her? It had been accidental at first, but he sure hadn't made a move to distance himself. His daughters were right; Maggie smelled like cinnamon. With her creamy skin hosting a highlight of freckles brought on by the spring sunshine, she looked ready to be featured in a lotion commercial. He shook his head. He really needed to stop thinking in Hollywood terms.

Kellen pushed away from the wall and took a step back. He crossed his arms.

Maggie straightened to her full height and lifted her chin. "Questions?"

Right. Questions. He'd wanted to ask her if she knew whether the house was lined with rock-wool insulation or fiberglass and see if the wooden paneling was attached to the studs or if it was the glued-on variety. But the words stuck in his mouth.

It was odd, seeing her without flour in her hair and in something more than ripped jeans and a T-shirt. Seeing her look so…put together. It made him feel unsteady. At the moment, he didn't know how to address her. People should stay the same all the time. It would make them so much easier for him to categorize.

He ran his tongue against the back of his teeth. "Why are you dressed like that?"

"Like what?" She smoothed her hands over the end of her shirt.

A thought hit him. "Do you have a date?"

"It's ten in the morning."

"Do you?" Why did it matter to him? She was a grown woman and there were no guests scheduled for the inn that evening. She was allowed to do whatever she wanted.

"Not today." She offered a tight-lipped smile.

"But you have a boyfriend?" Not that it was his business…

Her brow furrowed. "That's what you wanted to ask me?"

"No." He took a step back and bumped against the other

wall. The old hallways were so narrow. "I'm only asking because…I'm going to be around here a lot and will be paying attention to who is coming in and out of the inn now and don't want to mistake him for an intruder or something like that." *Good save.*

Maggie sighed. "Well, no worry there. I've reached confirmed-old-maid status in Goose Harbor. Believe me, I couldn't get a boyfriend if I paid someone." She winced as she spoke.

Old maid. No one used that term anymore, at least not seriously. Kellen searched her face before answering. Not that he knew her very well, but she didn't strike him as someone who said things for shock value. Or someone who belittled herself all the time for attention.

Maggie might be a gold digger. She might have used and manipulated his aunt, but she definitely wasn't mining for attention. He knew *that type* all too well. The attention-seeking women he'd known dressed flashy—provocatively. Wore pounds of makeup and turned heads as they teetered in high heels down the street and yet fished for compliments and ways to boost their self-esteem every chance they got. Thankfully Maggie was none of those things.

He lifted his back off the wall. "I may not know Goose Harbor well yet, but I know that can't be true. Let me guess— you've left a string of broken hearts all over town?"

"No." She shook her head as her cheeks flamed. "There's no one. There's been no one for…well, a very long time."

"How long?" Why was he pressing the issue? He needed to know. Right? In order to protect his inheritance, he had to get to the bottom of who Maggie West really was and why his aunt had protected her in the will. At least, that sounded like a good enough reason.

"I'll just catch you later, okay?" She swung past him, making a beeline for the staircase.

He caught her by the crook of the arm and turned her to face him. What he saw frayed his thoughts like a snapped guitar string in the middle of a concert. Twin paths of tears trailed down Maggie's face. And with her pale skin, the area around her eyes had already turned red.

She swiped at her cheeks with her palm.

"You wanted to talk to me about something else, didn't you? I got you off track." Kellen dropped his voice to an intimate level. It was the same way he spoke to Ruthy and Skylar when one of them was upset.

"It's fine." She sniffled and rubbed the back of her hand against her nose. "I'll touch base with you in an hour or so. Does that work?"

It did, but Kellen yearned for real emotion. Wanted to have a connection with someone, knowing everything being said was sincere, so much so that he couldn't let the poor, crying woman go. Had he actually ever had a real, honest and open conversation with anyone? Truthfully? Probably not.

No one wanted to know the real him—or be real with him—when his band was touring. They liked their image of him too much. But even before then, when he was a pastor's kid, his childhood and teenage years consisted of plastering on smiles and looking good for the church. No wonder he'd rejected his parents' faith for so long.

What had the counselor he'd met with back in California said to him? Something about his need to process "real moments" with a woman without feeling as though she only wanted something from him? It was a comment along those lines.

He guided Maggie to the window seat. "We're both here. Let's just talk now."

She stayed standing. "I thought you said it was rotted."

Was she trying to be sassy? Kellen bit back a smile.

"There's wood rot, but the seat will hold like it has been for the last hundred years." He patted the space beside him.

"I'm sure it's been replaced a couple times in a hundred years."

It wasn't a large area, but they both fit on the seat together. Maggie instantly tugged her legs up to sit cross-legged—like a kid on the floor during reading-circle time—on the seat, which made it so her knee rested against his thigh. She pressed her face into her hands.

Most men felt uncomfortable around tears—sure, he did, too. But Maggie had no reason to put up a front with him right now. As his counselor had instructed, he'd take the human connection for what it was, even if it was an uncomfortable one. If only to know he was still capable of connecting with other adults after everything he'd been through.

Kellen rested his hand between her shoulder blades and started to rub small circles against her back.

Maggie took a long breath. "Sorry. I'm being so stupid."

"You're not at all. Something I said bothered you, and you're allowed to be upset or frustrated."

"Seriously? I've never known a man to say something like that."

Kellen shrugged. "I have two daughters." She didn't say something right away, so he tried to fill the silence. "Anyway, there are four of us boys in my family, but even still, my mom used to always say that crying can be a good thing—even when it's brought on by a hard situation. She used to call it 'washing the soul.' I always liked that. Washing the soul doesn't seem like something to be embarrassed about. You know?"

She sat up finally, leaning her head against the window as she looked up at the ceiling. "It's just... What time is it?"

"A little after ten."

Quickly Maggie rose to her feet and rubbed her cheeks. She paced back and forth in the five feet of space in front of the window seat. She was Tasmanian Devil Maggie again— all fidgety motion.

What had her so worked up? They'd been seated together for only two or three minutes, but he already missed the connection. Kellen fought the urge to grab her hand, tug her back down beside him and wrap his arm around her.

She finally stopped and faced him. "I need money."

Kellen reeled back a bit as if someone had struck him. Because that was how it felt. Maggie had played him for a fool, and so easily. Was she so good at manipulating that he hadn't caught on?

Of course she wanted his money. With women, that was what it always came to. Cynthia and the other groupies hadn't really cared about him or his bandmates. They'd seen dollar signs and tagged along. That was all. Who he was hadn't mattered and it never would. That much was made plain when Cynthia had ditched their girls and jumped right over to the drummer of Snaggletooth Lions the second Kellen breathed a word about leaving the band.

Not to mention every woman since. That was why he'd given up dating altogether. Back in LA everyone still viewed him as the ex–lead singer of a successful, touring band. The couple women he'd dated in the past two years had done their research. Not that it took much—a simple internet name search showed the fact that he'd written every single one of the hit songs that the Snaggletooth Lions played. And a songwriter meant royalties.

Or so they all thought.

The second they learned he'd signed over all royalty rights to Cynthia and the band in exchange for full custody of his daughters, the women always left. Quickly. No one actually wanted Kellen Ashby. Just the money they thought he had hidden somewhere.

Kellen ground his molars together. Hard.

Maggie was no different. Just as Kellen had thought when he heard about her from the lawyer, Mr. Rowe. A couple well-timed tears and he'd dropped his guard.

Not again.

Chapter Five

Kellen's nostrils flared as he took three deep breaths.

"Money. That's what this display was about?" His laugh held no humor.

Display? Did he think...? Maggie jerked her head back. "Excuse me, but you're the one who was asking ridiculously personal questions and upsetting me. Not the other way around."

She'd foolishly let him comfort her. Wow. She'd almost spilled everything about Alan to him, too. A smile and a warm presence for a moment had made her forget that Kellen had, only days ago, been ready to throw away Ida's Bible. The man had no heart. She'd do well to remember that.

"You said you had some questions—were those all of them? Or did you also want to ask probing, hurtful questions about my mom's long illness and my sister's murder while you were at it? You know—nice, pleasant topics." She heard her voice rising and didn't care.

Kellen scrubbed his hand down his face. "Actually I didn't get to ask you any of the questions I wanted to."

"Well, ask away. 'Cause, buddy, you're on a roll."

"Another day." He stood, brushing past her.

She trailed him down the stairs. Oh! She fisted her hands so hard her nails bit into her palms. If he didn't hold the West Mansion—one of the last things she loved—in the palms of his hands, she would have said something unladylike and unkind to him.

He spun around when he reached the bottom, stopping her on the third-to-last step. "What do you want money for?"

She swallowed hard. "Food."

The angry lines around his mouth and eyes eased. "You don't have food?"

"We have three rooms booked as of tomorrow night. I need to replenish the inn's kitchen before then."

Kellen motioned for her to follow him into the kitchen in the private section of the inn. He rolled his shoulders and then flipped open his notepad. "Where do we order from?"

Maggie braced her hands on the butcher-block island. "Order what?"

"The food."

"It's Friday morning. I just head to the farmers' market in town. They host one on both Friday and Saturday from spring through fall."

"The inn gets its food from a farmers' market?" Kellen dropped onto a stool on the other side of the island. "Yikes."

Maggie shrugged. "There are laws keeping big-box and chain stores out of Goose Harbor, so we actually don't have a grocery store in town. I'd have to drive to Shadowbend, the next town over, to buy them there. It's easier to hop on my bike and get what we need from the market in town."

Rubbing his temples, Kellen made eye contact with her. "That can't be cost-effective."

"Buying our ingredients from the local market is part of the charm of the bed-and-breakfast. People come here expecting that the eggs in their omelet came from chickens on nearby farms. That we know the people who grew and picked the strawberries topping their pancakes. That—"

"Our own flesh and blood churned the butter." Kellen rolled his eyes. "People don't care about that kind of stuff. They care that it tastes good. Period." He pulled his phone from his pocket, set it on the counter and opened the internet. Probably checking to see if she was right about the grocery stores. "I'll locate a nearby food distributor that can get us our orders at a discount. We can come up with a set menu so we always know exactly how much we're spending."

A set menu? But what about their regulars? What about people who wanted to try new things? "We can't—"

"We can. It's what I used to do for the restaurant I managed."

He didn't get it. "No. I mean—"

"Maggie—"

She put her hands up. "Stop! Stop cutting me off every time I try to say something."

Kellen rubbed his jaw. "I was doing that. Wasn't I?"

"Constantly."

"I'm sorry."

She scooped a handful of crumbs off the counter and dumped them into the trash can. "Even if we start ordering at some point—" *Please. Please don't let that ever happen* "—that doesn't solve our problem today. We're out of food. We need more. And there's no money left."

"When you say no money left…?"

Maggie explained about the envelope and how Ida used to put more cash in it whenever it started getting low.

"Wait." Kellen tugged on his hair. "You're telling me there are no spreadsheets. No financial programs installed on the ancient computer in the office." He jutted his thumb in the direction of the back hallway. "Nothing tracking the money being spent to keep this inn running?"

"Not that I'm aware of."

"This is so much worse than I thought." He tugged his wallet from his jeans, opened it and handed her a stack of twenties. With the way he'd acted a few minutes ago, it was best to count the money later.

Maggie reached for the cash, but Kellen didn't release it.

His gaze locked with hers. "For right now." He let go. "We'll sit down together next week and figure out a better system. Deal?"

"Sure." Maggie slipped the money into her back pocket and rushed out the back door. She grabbed her bicycle and hopped on before Kellen had a chance to run outside and change his mind.

What if he turned the West Oaks Inn into a place she was no longer proud of? Would she leave? She couldn't let that happen.

A chill washed down her back as she turned off her residential street and pedaled toward the town square. One of the great things that made the old West Mansion a good bed-and-breakfast was it took only five minutes by bike or about fifteen minutes walking to make it to the downtown strip. The downtown area sat lower than the residential portion of town, which was built on the other side of the dunes.

Maggie tipped her head back a fraction, letting the cool spring air coming off the lake revitalize her. Today she wished the ride was longer. She would have liked more time to think. Process.

Outside of dropping his girls off at school and the Rowes', Kellen hadn't left his new property much. Maggie figured he hadn't talked to many people yet, but what if he had? What if news that she didn't own the inn already circulated in town? She'd have to be honest. She'd have to fess up to her friends that she'd lost her family home years ago and had kept it from them. If not now, the word would get out someday soon. She had to prepare herself for the questions. The disappointed looks.

As she got closer to town the street turned from concrete to brick. The original city planners of Goose Harbor had built it in a unique way. Instead of the normal main drag with businesses lining either side, Goose Harbor had a huge parklike square in the center of town with a street running around it. Businesses lined the square and then fanned out down the joining streets, making the town look like an octopus on the map.

Maggie wouldn't change a thing. She loved the huge square with its gazebo, park benches and rose garden. She loved that the heart of her city was planned with the intention that the residents would *want* to all join together for parties, civic functions and town traditions.

And Goose Harbor had many quirky traditions.

She left her bike lying in a parking spot next to a motorcycle she knew belonged to her friend Shelby's boyfriend, the fireman Joel Palermo. Joel wouldn't mind sharing the space. More likely than not, he'd find Maggie and pester her about not wearing a helmet.

Since Ida's funeral, Maggie had battled a drowning feeling in her soul. That feeling had intensified since Kellen moved in next door. With so much uncertainty piling up around her, it was hard to focus on the things that mattered in life. People. They had to come first or she'd lose hold of the purpose behind every sacrifice she'd ever made.

With each step toward the farmers' market, some weight fell from her shoulders. For the next twenty minutes, she could forget her problems and enjoy seeing her friends. There were fewer people gathered around the booths today because it was midday on a Friday. Most of them, Maggie's best friend, Paige, included, were currently at work. Tourists milled around the booths, oohing and aahing over local honey and fresh-cut flowers.

Maggie rounded the first row of tables, choosing to skip that aisle because it was dedicated to handmade knickknacks. She eased the money Kellen had given her out of her pocket and counted it. Two hundred dollars. Far more than she'd need for the couple food items she planned on grabbing today. How long did he expect the money to last? And how would he pay her? Ida had handed her cash twice a month as payment.

Although, after how Kellen had acted today, she wished she'd done the same with the money Ida gave for inn items. Maybe Ida had. Perhaps Kellen would find paperwork in Ida's house that detailed everything. If he hadn't already tossed her files.

Maggie stopped by the first booth in the second aisle. A banner suspended on poles behind it showed the Crest Orchards logo. The orchard lay on the edge of town, between Goose Harbor and Shadowbend, and held a reputation throughout the region for its quality produce. Last summer the booth had been manned by Mr. Crest, but today his only daughter smiled back at her.

"Hey, Jenna." Maggie wanted to skirt around the table and hug the girl. It had been a long time since she last saw her. Jenna Crest was almost ten years younger than Maggie. She had to be, because Maggie babysat her multiple times, many years ago. Jenna had blond curly hair that, unlike Maggie's curls, actually behaved and stayed in place.

Jenna reached across the table and squeezed her hand. "I'm so glad to see you. I've wanted to stop by your place, but you turned it into an inn since the last time I lived around here. I didn't know what door to use or if I could just stop by."

"You're always welcome."

"Careful. I just might take you up on that." Jenna winked.

"I hope you do." Maggie eyed all the produce on the table and ran through a few options for recipes in her head. While Kellen was worried about spending, she'd choose to prepare the easiest meals that called for the fewest ingredients. "Give me a few bunches of your best asparagus and a bag of those cherries I spot on your back table."

Jenna spun around and added a second bag of cherries into a white plastic bag along with the other items. "On the house."

"Don't tell your dad."

"Oh, for you, Daddy wouldn't mind." Jenna fished some change out of the large front pocket on the apron she wore. "Those are the first cherries of the season. So good. Winter here is pretty terrible, but I always remind myself those sweet cherries are worth all those dark, cold, snowed-in nights."

Of course, Jenna was talking about real seasons, but Maggie's mind wandered to the winter in her soul. Would there be fruit worth the wait on the other side of her struggles? More likely, her winter would never end.

"I'll have to write that down and remind myself of that when I'm shoveling my long driveway next winter."

Jenna propped her hands on the table and lowered her voice. "Word around town is that there's a young man who moved into Ida's old place. Is that true?"

Of course they knew about Kellen. A newcomer didn't stay a secret within the close-knit community. Jenna hadn't mentioned his name, though, so that was a good sign. She still had time before she had to be honest with everyone.

Maggie linked the bag around her wrist. "He's one of Ida's nephews."

Jenna waggled her eyebrows. "Maybe if you sweet-talk him, he'll all neighborly and shovel the drive for you."

Kellen probably would—seeing as the inn belonged to him. But Jenna didn't need to know that. For now, no one did.

"Do you know much about him? What's his name?" Jenna waved to her next customer and handed the man a bag of artichokes.

"Kellen Ashby."

"Kellen. That's a good name." Jenna tapped her chin. "Is that Irish? It sounds Irish."

"I don't know." Maggie shrugged. "He could be."

"Huh." Jenna leaned with her hip against the pole holding up the store sign. "His name sounds really familiar and I can't place why."

"Maybe Ida mentioned him to you."

"Perhaps." Jenna worked her bottom lip between her teeth as if she were taking a math quiz. "Oh well. It'll come to me at the oddest moment."

"I better head out." Maggie stepped away from the booth. "I have a couple more things to pick up and I still have to prepare the inn for some guests tomorrow."

Jenna held up a finger. "Shelby mentioned that she's starting a small group that meets at the new church on Thursday nights. Are you planning to go to it? I don't know everyone else as well as I know you, and I'd feel more comfortable if you're going to be there."

Maggie bit her tongue. She hadn't considered going. Not in the state that her heart was in right now. Currently she had some undealt-with anger at God, and going to a small group with that weighing on her sounded like the worst idea ever.

But if Jenna needed her, she should be there. Maggie forced a cheery smile—the one that had become her constant mask the past few years. "I'll see you on Thursday, then."

She'd do the right thing, but it wouldn't do her or her wounded heart any good.

Just as usual.

"Yes. Next Thursday at four it is. I'll be here." Kellen gave the home appraiser the address to both the cottage and the West Oaks Inn. Knowing how much each place was worth would help him prioritize improvement projects. Or get rid of them.

He was still waiting for a call back from Sandra Conner, an interior designer he'd contacted. Whenever she could meet, it wouldn't be soon enough. If he'd learned one thing while managing the five-star Casa Bonita, it was that a good design paid off every time.

Before meeting with the designer, he'd spend some time researching successful inns and bed-and-breakfasts to figure out what direction he should go in for the West Oaks Inn. Although anything would be better than the grandmotherly mash-up of items that filled the place currently.

Skylar slung open the back door. Right into Kellen's heel. He yelped.

Repeat, their little orange kitten, scurried to a hiding spot under the table at the noise.

Man, that hurt.

"Daddy? Are you okay? I'm sorry." She grabbed his shoulder as he crouched down to rub his foot.

"It's all right, sweetheart." He patted her hand as he stood. "It wasn't your fault. This place is just too small." And that was the crux of everything. He'd gone over his improvement notes for the West Oaks Inn more than twenty times as well as a list he'd made for the cottage. Almost everything needed updates—besides the appliances, which he'd replaced over the first weekend in town—but were they even worth doing? In a few years, the cottage would be way too small to house his girls and meet their needs. No, it already was.

What he needed to do was get Mr. Rowe to reread the will and possibly find a loophole for the Maggie situation. Did the will actually state that he had to let her live in the inn? Or did he just have to provide a place for her? He should have either listened better or packed his copy of the will with the initial stuff he'd brought with him instead of leaving it in a moving truck crossing the country. Now it was somewhere in the unpacked boxes in his bedroom.

Perhaps he could make Maggie swap the private side of the inn for the cottage. Where she lived was big enough for his family, and then some.

That or he could sell the inn outright. How much money would that bring in? And would that dissolve his responsibility where Maggie was concerned? He didn't want to kick her out onto the streets, but surely she had somewhere else to go. She was a grown woman who'd already proven she was completely capable of taking care of herself.

Moving to Goose Harbor was supposed to simplify his life, not make it more stressful. Maybe—like most of the other choices he'd made in the past ten years—he'd acted hastily and made a huge mistake by moving here.

Ruthy ambled in hanging on to Mrs. Rowe's hand. "Are we still going to the dunes?"

Kellen dropped back down to his knees and bear-hugged his youngest daughter. "Of course. I promised, right?"

She stared down at the tips of her shoes. "Sometimes that doesn't mean it'll happen."

His heart squeezed. Had he really gone back on his word

that many times in her short life? No matter what stress filled his days in Goose Harbor, the set of his youngest child's shoulders told him that leaving LA had been for the best. He never wanted to let his girls down again.

Kellen lifted her chin. "I haven't always followed through when I promised to do something with you before, have I?"

Ruthy's frown deepened.

"From now on, you can trust me. Okay? If I say we'll do something, we're going to do it." He looked up at Mrs. Rowe, who smiled down at them with grandmotherly affection. "Thanks again for watching her this past week. I'll figure something else out, but since we just arrived and don't know—"

Mrs. Rowe waved her hand, dismissing his words. "Say no more. I love spending time with your girls. Ruthy and I did play pedicure today. I hope you don't mind her having painted toes."

"Not at all."

"They're red, Dad. Wanna see?" Ruthy started yanking off her shoes.

"How about you go get changed for the dunes and you can show me there?" He pressed a kiss to her forehead before she and Skylar raced to their shared bedroom.

Minutes later he tossed a blanket into the trunk of his Subaru and called for the girls to hurry up.

Skylar bolted through the doorway first. "Hi, Maggie!" She waved wildly in the direction of the inn.

Ruthy bumbled after Skylar, dragging a towel behind her. He'd told her she wouldn't be swimming. It was only spring in Michigan; the water in the Great Lake wouldn't be warm enough by now. The girls didn't understand that Lake Michigan wasn't the same as swimming in the ocean. She'd still try to convince him again once they got there.

Kellen pivoted so he could see his neighbor. Maggie

had been hunched over weeding in one of her many garden areas near the picket fence that ran the length of the
property. She had different garden spaces along walking
paths all over the grounds of the bed-and-breakfast.

He hadn't talked to her since their tense discussion about
money the day before. Thinking back, he'd reacted stronger than he should have. Again. How he spoke to her...
Treat others better than yourself. It hadn't been right, no
matter what the situation.

Maggie walked to the gate. "Hey, Skylar. Good to see
you."

Skylar skipped up to meet Maggie. "Do you want to come
to the beach with us?"

The innkeeper scrunched up her eyebrows. "It's a little
cold yet for the beach, isn't it?"

Kellen joined them near the fence and rested his hands
on the top rung. Maggie had her head turned in a way
where she was paying attention to only Skylar.

Skylar slipped her hand into Kellen's. "Dad says we're
not allowed to go in the water."

Still looking at only Skylar, Maggie pulled off her gardening gloves. "I have to agree with him this one time."

"Only this one time?" Kellen laughed and he finally drew
her gaze.

"Let's just say, Mr. Ashby, I'm going to take a wild
guess that you and I don't have much in common." Maggie nodded to acknowledge him.

"Whoa. What's with the formal greeting?"

"You are my boss, aren't you?"

Technically he was. Or something along those lines. He
hadn't minded the term or formality when he was the manager of a crowd of staff at the restaurant, but with it being
only one person it didn't feel right. "'Kellen' is just fine.

And as for not having much in common, I think you're wrong."

"Oh." Her eyebrows darted up. "Is that so?"

"We both care about the future of the inn, we're both stubborn and we both love the Lord." He ticked off the ways on his fingers as he spoke. "How's that for common ground?"

Maggie tucked her gloves into her back pockets and dusted off her knees. "Well, have a great time at the dunes."

Skylar bounced beside him. "You should come with us."

Now it was Maggie's turn to laugh, and her laughter was beautiful. Full. So many women tried to cover their mouth or temper their laughs, but not Maggie. She tossed her head back. "I don't think that's the best idea, honey. Your dad and I aren't the best of friends and it's a family thing. You guys go on and have fun."

Kellen cleared his throat. "You should join us."

"Really?" Maggie patted her curls. "It's probably best if I—"

Ruthy, who'd been twirling her towel around in circles a few feet away, let out a scream. Maggie's eyes grew wide and then she turned to run back toward the inn.

"Oh, Ruthy." Kellen dropped Skylar's hand to kneel beside Ruthy. He smoothed his hand over her mess of light red hair and she started crying harder. "Did you fall?"

"Yessss." Ruthy clutched her leg.

The scrape wasn't bad, but Ruthy had always been the more sensitive of his two girls. He'd wondered before if it was because she'd never known a mother's love. She'd been less than a year old when Cynthia walked away from them.

Kellen tried to be everything for the girls, but men and women thought and processed so differently. Would he be enough for them when they were teenagers with all sorts of life questions? No. But he'd have to be.

Skylar plopped onto the ground on the other side of Ruthy, her chin in her hands. She looked on the verge of tears, as well. "Does this mean we can't go to the beach? We never get to do anything fun."

From out of nowhere, Maggie dropped down beside Kellen and clicked open a little first aid kit. That was what she must have run to the inn for. Why hadn't he thought of that?

"Everyone's going to be all right and you'll still go to the beach. I promise."

Maggie pulled out an alcohol swab. "This will sting for a second, but you're super brave, right?"

Ruthy scooted onto Kellen's lap as he mouthed *Thank you* to Maggie.

Making quick work of the doctoring process, Maggie cleaned Ruthy's knee, put some antibacterial cream on it and topped it with a Band-Aid. Much more attention than the scrape required, but Ruthy's tears ebbed to a stop and Kellen was thankful for that.

Kellen squeezed Ruthy in a tight hug while Maggie clipped her first aid kit shut. "I think we should say a quick prayer before we all head out." He pulled Skylar close to his side and draped an arm around Maggie, bowing his head so that his forehead rested on top of Ruthy's head. "Lord, thank You for today, for my family and for Your constant provisions. I've noticed lately how much You're a part of every moment of our lives and I'm sorry I was blind to that for a long time. Please watch over us as we head to the dunes, and thank You for sending Maggie to save us from medical emergencies twice now. We ask these things in Your Son's name. Amen."

He squeezed Skylar's and Maggie's shoulders in unison as he ended and then stood, picking up Ruthy. "Let's head out."

Skylar whooped and ran toward the car. She was in and buckled before he could get to the other side of the car to secure Ruthy into her booster seat.

Maggie trailed after him. "Well, you guys have fun."

He finished buckling Ruthy, closed the door and then stepped toward Maggie. "Aren't you coming?"

She laced her fingers together and cocked her head to the side. "You actually want me to come? You weren't just saying that?"

"Yes, to the 'I want you to come with us' part." The answer surprised him just as much as her. "Are you kidding me? We need you in order to avoid tragedy at the dunes." He winked.

After everything, Kellen didn't trust his ability to read people well, so he needed more time with Maggie if he was going to be able to pin down who she was and what she was after. Had she preyed on his elderly aunt? Or was she in the midst of unfortunate circumstances herself?

She'd almost admitted something to him the other day. He'd have to convince her to open up to him again.

Chapter Six

"I probably shouldn't have come along." Maggie cradled a basket of food on her lap as Kellen turned his car away from the residential part of town and down the winding country road that led to the nature preserves and beaches that lined Lake Michigan. "I have so much to do before more guests show up tomorrow."

"It'll get done." At a stop sign, Kellen fiddled with his MP3 player until some cartoon princess began to sing through the car's speakers. From the backseat two little voices joined in.

Maggie traced the twine that laced the pieces of the basket together. "I sure hope so."

Kellen pressed his lips together, almost as though he was trying not to laugh. "It's okay not to work all the time."

"True. But when there are things to get done…" Maggie drummed her fingers on the top of the basket. What foolishness, joining the Ashbys. She had bedsheets to wash and iron and bathrooms to clean and floors to scrub back at the inn.

Catching her by surprise, Kellen leaned over and rested his hand on top of hers, stopping her fidgeting. "Not that long ago, I was a workaholic. To the point where I missed out on everything. I was getting by, paying bills—but it wasn't living. Does that make sense?"

He still had his hand cupped over hers. Maggie's pulse swirled like her KitchenAid on its highest mixing setting.

When she didn't speak, Kellen removed his hand, placing both of them on the wheel again. "God wants us to do our work as if we're working for Him. Having a good work ethic is an admirable thing. But overworking—not letting yourself enjoy the world He's created and placed us in—well, that's not good, either. I have no clue what the correct balance is, but these days I believe in stopping to enjoy my blessings. At least…I'm learning to."

Skylar leaned forward in her seat. "Sing along, Daddy!"

"Oh. I don't know if we should subject Maggie to a spectacle like that."

"Pleaeeze." Skylar clasped her hands together. "You sing the best."

Maggie laughed. "Sounds like you better join them."

Kellen expelled a theatrical groan. "If the ladies insist."

And then he started to sing. It might have been only a silly song from a television cartoon about a princess deciding if she was ready to become a ruler—but Kellen sounded like a dreamy Disney prince. His voice was rich and clear. Better than half of the musicians who filled the CDs that Maggie owned. She wanted to close her eyes, lean back against the seat and smile. He had that type of voice.

Unaware of the special talent their dad possessed, his daughters in the backseat belted out the words with unmatched gusto.

Back in the yard a few minutes ago, she hadn't at first been tempted to join the Ashbys on their adventure, but then Kellen had wrapped his arm around her and pulled her into their prayer circle. Such a simple, friendly gesture. One that had probably meant nothing to Kellen. But to Maggie—for the first time in a long while—she'd felt as though she belonged. He'd wanted to include her and wasn't just doing it because she happened to be a third wheel along for the ride.

She had tried to pack away her dreams of a family. Locked the wish up tight in an old chest in her heart and tossed the key. The days of hoping for a husband and longing for children were gone. Time had passed her by while she was tending to her aging grandma and sick mother.

Yet in the car as she listened to Kellen and his girls, the dream almost felt attainable again. If she couldn't have a family of her own, perhaps she could grow old next door to Skylar and Ruthy. Sure, it wouldn't have the marriage part. No. A man like Kellen would never settle for a woman like her. Why was she even thinking about him in that light?

Maggie stole a glance his way.

With one arm perched on the open window and a hand hooked around the steering wheel, he looked over at her again. Their stares collided, and Maggie's breath caught. Kellen was handsome. Ten times more handsome than any of the other men in Goose Harbor. Most men who'd grown up in the area were strong and semi-woodsy, like her friend Caleb Beck. But Kellen was different. Lean, but still manly. With his lopsided grin and spiking blond hair, he looked more like a male model found in catalogues for expensive clothing. A heavy peacoat and scarf wouldn't look out of place on him.

And then there was that voice…

"Sing with us." He winked again.

Breathe, Maggie.

"I…I don't know the song." Her gaze broke with his and skittered to look out the window.

That was the crux of everything, wasn't it? *I don't know the song.* What did she know of love and romance? Nothing. That was what. By Goose Harbor standards she was a confirmed spinster who just needed to adopt four or five cats in order to seal the deal.

Besides, a guy like Kellen probably wanted a woman who knew how to wear makeup and didn't constantly have some sort of batter caked under her nails. Maggie was hopeless when it came to that. Or styling her curls.

A beautiful voice, caring attitude with his daughters, capable business mind with the inn and cute smile couldn't erase the fact that he hadn't cared about Ida and her Bible. Moreover, he was Maggie's boss and he held the power to ruin her life and destroy the only link she had left to her family.

She had no control over those things. Not at the moment. As Kellen suggested, she could let go of those things—for now—and simply enjoy the drive and the fresh air for the next hour.

Midafternoon sunshine played peekaboo through the waxy leaves that covered the towering oak trees lining the streets. How did trees that large survive in the sandy soil along the lake? Their roots dove so deeply into the earth that they'd become permanent fixtures.

Local history said that there used to be a town bordering the southern edge of Goose Harbor. An old logging community—Glen Hollow. More than a hundred years ago, the people there had taken down most of the trees and sold the wood to the people of Chicago after the great fire that totaled much of that city. The people of Glen Hollow had become wealthy, and in their desire for more, they took down the rest of the trees. Without roots holding the dunes in place, the sand began to take over the town. Little by little, the dunes shifted—covering homes, businesses… everything. The once prosperous Glen Hollow had to be abandoned. These days a dune-buggy business owned the town, and tourists piled into their vehicles and used the huge dunes like roller coasters.

Was she like the tall oaks of Goose Harbor? Unmoving, ready to hold strong as the world changed around her. Or was she poor Glen Hollow? So shaped by uprooted dreams and long-gone connections that she'd become completely lost in life? Surviving the worst only to exist, while the people around her enjoyed the ride that was their lives.

If only Maggie knew.

"Stay close where I can see you. Don't wander near the water. Understand?" Kellen tugged off Ruthy's shoes so she could wiggle her toes in the sand.

"See?" Ruthy wiggled her painted toes.

"Very pretty." Kellen squeezed her ankle.

Skylar nodded enthusiastically. "We'll be safe, Dad. Promise. We just want to build a castle."

"All right. You've got a half hour and then we're going to head back."

"I like it here. We never had fun before." Ruthy inched across the picnic blanket to hug him quickly before taking off after her older sister.

A few feet away on the picnic blanket, Maggie collected the uneaten food and tucked it back into the basket she'd brought along. After she'd agreed to join them, she'd jogged over to the inn and returned a few minutes later carrying a basket full of food, drinks, a Frisbee for the girls and a blanket. Maggie always thought ahead. Kellen liked that about her. He wasn't used to being around someone who constantly considered how to make the people around her comfortable. That quality made her a great innkeeper. If only she'd apply the same forethought to the business side of things, but that was where he came in—they had the potential to be an unstoppable team.

That was, if she didn't turn out to be an inheritance hunter. Even now, was she trying to get close to him?

But he couldn't believe that about her. Not now. Not after she'd given Ruthy a piggyback ride for the entire quarter-mile walk through the woods to get to the dunes. Not after she'd cut the crust off Skylar's bread and played along with his girls' games while they ate.

His daughters glowed under her attention. Skylar and Ruthy weren't used to a woman devoting time to them. Besides his sister-in-law and his mother, the other women who'd been in his life in LA ignored his daughters. Or acted annoyed by them.

He'd keep his guard up for sure, but watching Maggie smile as she kept a maternal eye on Skylar and Ruthy made his mission very difficult.

The food tucked away, Maggie pulled one of her legs up beside her and raised her eyebrows in his direction. "What did Ruthy mean when she said they never had fun before?"

Kellen sighed. In a heartbeat he was back in a chair, sitting with his old counselor. *Open up, Kellen. You'll have to trust someone, someday.*

He could give Maggie a bit of his story. Sharing was one of the quickest ways to get the other person to start talking. And that was what he needed, right? A better handle on Maggie. Telling his story could be a means to an end. He wouldn't need to give all the details, just enough.

He ran his fingers through his hair. Even giving the CliffsNotes version would prove hard. "Like I said in the car, I used to work a lot."

"At a restaurant—is that right?" Maggie pulled up her other leg and wrapped her arms around them.

And as a member of a touring band. Did she really not know? If she didn't, that was great—freeing. But he couldn't push away the sting of knowing Ida had never talked about him. Must not have been proud of him as she was his brothers. Why had she left him the house? *Pity.* It had to have been for pity only.

"Yes." He swallowed and looked out over the water. The lake was stiller than the ocean tides he'd grown used to. He liked the calmer waters. And the whole *no sharks* part. "I managed a five-star restaurant in Los Angles for the past two years. On a slow week, it was a sixty-hour-a-week position. Needless to say, I didn't see the girls all that often and when I did I was dead tired. I'm ashamed that they've spent a lot of their life in various day-care facilities."

Maggie rested her chin on her knee and stared at him for a long time. Her gaze moved from his hair to his eyes to his mouth. When she studied him, did she find him lacking?

"What happened to their mother?" Her voice was so soft.

Kellen straightened his spine. He should have known that question was coming.

Dropping her arms from around her legs, Maggie turned to face him fully. "I shouldn't have… You don't have to answer that."

"It's fine." Kellen brushed his hands together, clearing sand that wasn't there. "Their mother left us."

With a sharp intake of breath, Maggie reached over and touched his forearm. "I'm so sorry."

He shrugged. "I'm not. Is that terrible?" He shook his head. "Cynthia never loved me. I thought she did—but I was young and blinded and she was very beautiful. You have to understand, I wasn't walking with the Lord when I met her. Probably the furthest thing from that."

Maggie scrunched her eyebrows together as if she were working out a difficult math puzzle, but her hand stayed where it rested on his arm. "I thought you said your father was a minister."

The wind had picked up some since they arrived at the dunes. Sand peppered the breeze and scratched its way across his bare feet.

"He was—*is*. But I'd rejected everything he believed in." Kellen shifted, breaking contact with her. "Growing up in a minister's house, you have this pressure to be perfect. And, Maggie, I'm not perfect. I dreamed of doing things with my life that my father's congregation wouldn't have approved of. I resented that I had to live under the microscope of the church. It was always 'you can't do that,' 'you can't say that.' 'What will the elders think?'"

He scooped up a handful of sand and let it trickle between his fingers. "So at eighteen I ran away and ended up in Hollywood like every other starry-eyed teenager. You can imagine how my life was there. The people I spent my time with. The parties I went to."

Unable to stop fidgeting, Kellen stood. "When I met Cynthia I really thought my life was on the path I'd always wanted it to be, so it felt like being with her was right. If that makes any sense. I wanted to prove that everything my parents believed was wrong. That *they* were wrong." He walked a few feet away and turned his back to Maggie. "Then I started noticing how Cynthia would flirt with other guys. I wrote it off at first. Told myself she was just being outgoing. But I caught her doing more than flirting too many times to count. We already had two kids, though, so I tried to make it work." He turned to face her. "Kids are supposed to have a mom. Except she was never a nurturing mother."

He met Maggie's gaze as she looked up at him and didn't find any judgment there. It was odd, how she didn't jump in to talk or condemn him or change the subject—those were the normal responses he got with women. But Maggie was leaning forward, interested in hearing his story.

How refreshing.

He hooked his hand on the back of his neck and paced. "Life got…dangerous for my daughters, and I decided to make a change."

Dangerous was putting it lightly. He'd never forget the day Ruthy learned to walk. Finding her toddling around the tour bus with a used syringe in her hand had sent him into a panic. Even now, if he thought about it too much it made him nauseated. If he'd found her a minute later… In all his time playing with the Snaggletooth Lions, Kellen had never ventured into drug use, but the rest of the band had become addicts.

At least that one lesson from his childhood had remained strong.

The second he discovered Ruthy like that, he'd scooped up both her and Skylar and packed their bags. He couldn't endanger his daughters any longer. Achieving a dream wasn't worth it. Growing up under the pressure of the church was better than them seeing drug abuse, wild parties and their mother crawling out of his band members' beds.

He'd told Cynthia they were leaving and she laughed in his face. Called him a fool. Two days of trying to talk sense into her ended with her declaring love for the band's drummer and shoving legal paperwork in his face. All her parental rights turned over for all his rights to the royalties.

Easiest decision of his life.

"Their mother refused to come with us. She's bent on continuing with a lifestyle I'm not okay with exposing the girls to."

Maggie braced her hands on the ground. "Are you still in love with her?"

He jerked his head back. "Cynthia? No." Kellen dropped back down next to Maggie on the blanket. "Honestly I never was. I know that sounds terrible. She was exciting and she seemed to worship the ground I walked on, and to a young man, that sounded appealing. But I didn't know what love was back then."

Down on the beach, Ruthy shrieked happily as Skylar chased after her with a clump of seaweed.

"But you do now?" Maggie whispered.

"I'd like to think so." He watched Skylar and Ruthy as they shuffled in circles around the castle they'd built, giggling as though they didn't have a care in the world. "Two years ago I showed up on my parents' doorstep with my daughters in my arms and begged for their forgiveness. It was like the prodigal-son story all over again. They took me back without a second thought. Then as a twenty-seven-year-old man I took my dad's hand and asked him to pray with me so I could become a Christian."

That was enough. It would have to be, because telling even just that had drained him.

Maggie jutted her chin in the direction of his daughters. "It looks like they bounced back." Then she bumped her shoulder into his. "You will, too."

Kellen shuffled his heels against the sand like a nervous kid. "I don't need to bounce. These days I prefer having both feet planted on solid ground. Safe. That's all I want." He bumped her back with his shoulder. "Enough about me. What about Miss Maggie West?"

Only by a fraction, but he felt Maggie stiffen beside him.

"There isn't much to tell."

"I'm sure that's not true."

"What do you want to know?"

"Why aren't you married?"

Maggie ran her fingers over the lines on the picnic blanket. "No one ever wanted me."

Kellen pulled away to get a better read on her face.

"Someone as caring and hardworking as you? I don't believe that." Sure, he questioned her motives about Ida, but he couldn't deny how much she did for the guests at the West Oaks Inn, or how tirelessly she served people to the point of her missing out on sleep and fun for herself. Even today, she'd debated not coming to the beach in order to continue working. Maggie had drive.

She let out a long stream of air. "I've only dated one man. One chaste relationship in my entire life. Pathetic, huh? He grew up in Goose Harbor, but we didn't get to know each other until we were in our twenties. When everyone else left for college, I stayed home to take care of my mother and my grandmother, and Alan stuck around because college wasn't for him."

"Because he wanted to be by you?"

"No." She laughed, once, clipped. "We weren't dating when he did that. Alan's an artist. He never felt like he needed school in order to succeed." She rolled her eyes when she said "artist."

Good thing he hadn't talked about his music.

Kellen shifted. "So, what happened?"

Maggie shoved hair out of her face. "He eventually left Goose Harbor and I stayed. End of story."

"Did you love him?" Why had he asked that? Just to toss her question back at her? No. The hurt etching Maggie's voice piqued his curiosity. Did Maggie still pine for this Alan guy?

"I don't know. I thought so at the time. But what do I know of love?" She laced her fingers together and stared down at where they joined. Wind whipped her curls in all directions, making her look wild—no, free. "My first date ever was at age twenty-three. I shouldn't even tell you stuff like that. It's embarrassing. It wasn't love—at least, nothing close to what I imagine love to be. I was thrilled to have someone pay me a little attention, tell me my hair isn't all that bad and hand me flowers every once in a while."

Maggie was pure. Completely.

Kellen scooted away a few inches, afraid the dirtiness that was his past might tarnish her. "You deserve to be romanced. You know that, right? You deserve someone to tell you you're beautiful and worth sticking around for."

She shook her head hard enough to cause neck strain. "I'm not foolish. I don't need to be given a pep talk like I'm one of your daughters."

"I wasn't giving a pep talk. From what I've seen so far, you're a decent person, Maggie, and someone will notice that someday, and when you least expect it, love will knock on your door."

A smile slowly took over her face. "There you go, sounding like Ida. She always believed love would come my way, but it's not like we get an influx of new people in Goose Harbor all the time. Tourists, sure. But they leave too quickly."

"I'm new." Spotting some sand clinging to her cheek, Kellen had to chuckle. Maggie always had something on her. At first, the trait had bothered him—why couldn't she slow down and take more time with things when she was cooking or gardening? Didn't she care? But he'd come to realize that was exactly the issue—Maggie cared so much that she tossed herself into things entirely. Lost herself.

With the backs of his fingers he leaned over and brushed the sand from her face.

Maggie's breath caught as his fingertips glanced over the soft skin on her jawline. She had the deepest eyes, so full of compassion. Kellen's gaze landed on her lips. He drew closer. A breath away.

"Dad, I'm pretty hungry." Skylar's voice made him jump. "I know we had snacks, but I want some more."

As if he were a teenager again getting caught by his father cuddling with a girl, Kellen backed away from Maggie. He tapped his watch and hopped to his feet. "Yup, it's been a half hour. Time to head out."

They gathered the picnic blanket and Maggie picked up Ruthy again. He fell into step behind them as everyone headed back toward the parking lot.

He was a mess. After two years of trying to grow in his faith and become a man of quality, he'd almost kissed a woman he hardly knew. One he wasn't sure he even trusted. And why? Because they'd shared an honest moment and opened up about old wounds. Did he need to feel close to someone that badly?

Even if he felt a draw to Maggie, she'd never want him and all his baggage. Someone with so many mistakes to his name didn't deserve a happy ending. Not the way Maggie did. She'd lived a good life, been faithful to caring for her family and probably hadn't compromised herself with the one guy she'd dated.

People like Maggie got happy endings. Not him.

Unless she made it all up.

He stopped walking.

No. She wouldn't do that, would she? Was Maggie truly what she seemed, or was she being kind to him and his girls because he held her future in his hands? Because she had something to gain?

Chapter Seven

Maggie's stomach grumbled as they pulled up the driveway.

"See?" Skylar tapped Maggie's shoulder. "She's hungry, too. What's for dinner?"

Kellen put the car in Park, unbuckled his seat belt and then turned in his seat to catch Maggie's attention. "Should we order pizza?"

"Um." Maggie bit her lip as her mind swirled with conflicting thoughts.

Kellen hated Ida's home and didn't want to honor her memory—but Maggie was finding it hard to dislike him after he'd shared so openly at the beach. With the new information, she considered him a capable and brave man. But he could still ruin all her dreams. She'd placed her hopes in a man once. Look how well that had gone. Alan had walked off with not only her hopes, but all her money. Everything. She'd been so foolish to believe he'd pay her back...to trust.

She wouldn't—couldn't—let down her walls again. Even for friendship. She had to guard her heart. Like always.

It was all she had left to claim as hers.

She pushed the unlock button on the door and opened it. "I'll have to pass. There's so much to do. I shouldn't have even come with you guys. We have guests tomorrow." Climbing out of the car, she tripped a little and caught herself on the door.

"Careful." Kellen jogged around the front of the car to meet her. "Want me to carry the basket and blanket over?"

Behind him, Skylar helped Ruthy out of her seat.

Maggie walked backward. "There are beds to strip and sheets to wash and iron. Bathrooms to clean. Food to prep."

Kellen eased the basket out of her hands. "Sounds like a pizza for sure, then."

They were following her across the yard. Didn't they understand that she had work to do? "I can't."

"You can." Kellen opened the gate for her and made a sweeping gesture, welcoming her to keep walking.

No one ever got it. Maggie had so much to do. So much to juggle on her own. That was why she had only a few close friends in town. Good friends—but no one who stopped to help her. They'd invite her to their parties. Ask her over for a meal. But Maggie turned them down time after time in order to work around the inn, and their invites had become fewer and more spaced apart until some vanished altogether.

She climbed her porch and footsteps creaked behind her. Maggie spun around, making Kellen bump into her.

Maggie sidestepped him and squatted to be at eye level with Skylar and Ruthy. "Girls, there are some cookies in the Tupperware container sitting on the kitchen island. Go ahead and help yourself."

Ruthy grinned. "Can I have two?"

"Sure." Maggie smiled back as both girls rushed inside.

Still holding the basket and a blanket draped over his arm, Kellen leaned against the porch railing. "Why do I feel like this doesn't bode well for me?"

She faced him. "Listen. I had a nice time at the dunes. Thank you for inviting me."

He pushed off the railing and closed the distance between them in two steps, placing the basket and blanket on one of the chairs that lined the porch. "Is that your default when you're scared? The formality?" He tilted his head and lifted an eyebrow.

Never one to back down, Maggie crossed her arms. "This has nothing to do with being afraid. I was raised correctly, so I was attempting to politely ask you to leave."

His eyebrows dove. "Ask me to leave?"

"I have so much to get done and I can't push back those responsibilities any longer or else I'm going to be up until one in the morning, and no one wants a grumpy innkeeper greeting guests tomorrow."

"You don't have to do everything alone."

"Don't you see—I do." Maggie dropped her arms and balled her hands at her sides. No one got it. No one ever understood how alone she was in everything. "If I don't do it, no one else will. There's just me. There's always just been me. I'm stuck taking care of everything, so if you'll just excuse me—"

He grabbed her arm as she tried to turn and leave, gently pulling her back to face him. "Maggie, wait—"

Okay, now she was more than frustrated with Kellen. Maggie jerked away from his touch. "Don't you want the place looking its best for your guests tomorrow?"

Kellen raised his hands in surrender. "I'm trying to offer you help."

She narrowed her eyes. "Why would you want to help me?"

"Why wouldn't I?" He stepped around her and opened the back door. "The inn is mine, after all."

Ah. So there was his reason. Not because he wanted to

ease Maggie's load, but—like with the office—he wanted to have his hands in everything that happened at the inn.

He wanted control.

Maggie brushed past him into the kitchen. Fine. She'd take his help and give him the worst jobs. Why not? He was offering, after all.

Kellen pulled out his cell phone. "What's the best pizza place in town?"

"You don't have to order." Maggie had grabbed the basket off the back porch and started unpacking it. She had a few recipes for one-pot dinners. If the girls liked noodles she could make one of those. "I'll make something."

He leaned around her and pulled the cloth napkins out of the basket, his arm brushing hers in the process. "You just said we have a lot to do. Making dinner will only push us further behind." He tossed the napkins and blanket into a hamper she kept on the hall floor. "What kind of pizza do you like?"

Maggie ran her fingertips over the goose bumps that had broken out on the skin he'd just touched. "Anything besides olives."

They got the girls settled in the living room with a board game and cups of apple juice and silently went to work cleaning the kitchen side by side. Without being asked, Kellen unloaded the dishwasher, reloaded it and filled the sink so he could scrub the couple pots she'd left soaking. Maggie filled a bucket with the supplies she'd need to make sure the bathrooms in the three rooms the guests would be using were clean.

She looped two heavy buckets on her arms and grabbed a mop in one hand and a broom in the other. Sweat trickled down her spine and she hadn't started the real work yet. As she moved to back out of the kitchen into the public part of the inn, Kellen turned around, wiping his hands on a dish towel.

He rounded the island. "What else do you— Do you want me to help you carry that stuff upstairs?"

"No." She pulled the buckets close. "I'm fine. I do this all the time."

"It's just—"

"I'm fine." Maggie's arms shook. She tried to reposition the buckets so the handles weren't cutting into her skin so much.

"All right." Kellen pressed his lips together, obviously wanting to say more. "What's next for me to do?"

"Start a load of laundry and straighten the main areas where the guests spend time. They should be fine, but just spot-check the lobby and dining room." She pushed back against the door.

"And after that?" He followed her into the public area and then smiled. "You did say we had a lot to do."

"All the sheets will need to be ironed before we can dress the beds. That sort of thing." Before he could ask anything else, Maggie retreated up the stairs and went to work scrubbing and mopping. She should have done all these chores the other day after the previous guests left, but there had been a to-do list a mile long full of other things. Would she always be behind? It would appear so. In both innkeeping and life. No. When it came to life, it seemed she was on an entirely different path from her peers.

A path to nowhere.

Forty minutes later Kellen hollered from downstairs that the pizza had arrived. Maggie finished everything in the final room, so the only chore left was to make the beds. She trudged down the stairs, feeling tired and shaky. After dinner she'd have to start ironing—her most dreaded task.

She entered the kitchen and tucked the buckets away in a closet she used for storing linens and cleaning supplies and then joined the Ashbys at the kitchen table. Skylar and Ruthy were already chomping down on their second pieces of pizza.

Kellen passed a plate across the table. "Sorry, I couldn't get them to wait."

"No worries." Maggie dropped down into her seat and started eating. She rolled her shoulders once. So sore, and still more work to go. When would she get to sleep?

As she reached for a drink she noticed a bunch of pressed sheets draped over the back of the couch. "Are those ironed?"

Kellen set down his cup. "I didn't know which ones you wanted, so I ironed them all. I hope that's okay."

All of them?

"You didn't have to do that." Maggie blinked back tears. *Get a grip!* Why was she being so emotional about some ironed sheets?

He shrugged. "I like ironing. It's relaxing."

Shaking away her thoughts, Maggie played with the napkin on her lap. "No one likes ironing."

"My mom used to make me in high school. I got pretty good at it and don't mind the task." He put another piece of pizza on Skylar's plate. "It's better than the alternative. Believe me, I went through an all-wrinkled, grunge phase. It wasn't pretty."

The four of them chatted through dinner, and then Maggie dished up ice cream. Skylar talked nonstop about her class and teacher and the girl she played with at recess. Ruthy was quieter, but she kept glancing over to Maggie and smiling. Maggie wanted to pull them both onto her lap and hug them silly. Her heart squeezed. How could their mother not want to know them?

Once the girls were comfortable in the living room again, Maggie let them choose one of her G-rated movies to put in. Kellen retreated to the office and Maggie started food prep in the kitchen. The occasional giggle from the living room mixed with the sounds of her wooden spoon clanging against metal bowls as she stirred and the praise-and-worship music Kellen must have pulled up on the computer.

Maggie slipped a pan into the oven and then pressed out the back door. Dropping down on one of the steps, she cradled her head in her hands. She couldn't take hearing the sounds inside the inn any longer. Not because the girls giggling and Kellen singing along as he worked bothered her—the opposite. It all sounded like home. Like a family relaxing together.

Like the future she'd never have.

The tinkle of bells as Maggie finished dusting the last public room the next morning let her know that someone had just entered the inn's front door and was waiting for her downstairs. Looked as though the guests had decided to show up early. Talk about cutting it close.

She ditched the duster in an upstairs closet and adjusted her shirt and hair in a bathroom mirror before quickly going downstairs. In the lobby, a young woman dressed in jeans, heels and a suit coat waited with a tablet in her hands. Probably selling something.

Maggie smoothed her shirt. "Hello?"

The woman wore a too-big smile. "This place is just charming, now, isn't it?" She stuck out her hand. "Sandra Conner. It's so wonderful to meet you."

There was no Sandra Conner on her guest list.

Maggie shifted her weight to her other foot. "May I help you?"

Sandra puckered her lips. "Oh dear. I guess Mr. Ashby didn't tell you I'd be stopping by. I'm an interior designer. He hired me to give the inn the sprucing up it needs." Sandra sidestepped Maggie and did a few circles in the lobby. "Good height in here. Nice wood. Yes. I can make this place shine."

The sound of a car on Ida's old rock driveway sent Maggie outside. Sandra could poke around for herself while Maggie dealt with Kellen. She'd watched him load up the girls fifteen minutes ago. He must have dropped Skylar off at school and left Ruthy with Mrs. Rowe again.

Kellen closed the door on his Subaru and waved at her. "Morning."

He'd been so disarming and kind last night, helping with chores and playing the loving father with his girls. And now... *Cool down, Maggie.* She'd seen the care he used on his two separate trips back to his house last night, cradling each of his sleeping daughters. He *was* a loving father. He could be that and yet also be callous about the inn, right? They didn't negate each other.

Maggie barreled around the fence that separated their yards. "The inn is fine how it is."

Kellen pulled back his chin. "Okay?"

"There's a woman inside right now who said you're paying her to change everything." Maggie thrust her hand in the direction of the inn.

"Sandra's here already? That's great." Kellen grabbed a leather messenger bag from inside his car and motioned for Maggie to join him as he walked back to the inn.

She stayed where she was. "Did you hear me? The inn is perfect already."

When Ida had suggested turning the West Mansion into a bed-and-breakfast, she allowed Maggie to help decide how much of the old home would remain and how much would be changed in the needed remodeling. For the most part, besides a few rooms being changed into bathrooms so that all guest rooms had private facilities, and then squaring off the private area of the inn, the home had retained much of its old walls and feeling.

Kellen wouldn't think to ask her what walls she was okay with taking down or if it bothered her to lose more of the original setup of the home. He could change it all. Make it completely different. She'd endured enough change already. How could Maggie handle any more?

"It's not." Kellen shook his head and pulled some paperwork out of his bag. "I've been researching what makes an inn successful and what vacationers look for when they're booking a bed-and-breakfast." He tried to hand her the paperwork.

Maggie dropped her hands, refusing to look at them. "We always have guests. There's nothing wrong with the West Oaks Inn." In fact, everything about it was right. Maggie had spent the past five years scrounging through antiques fairs and estate sales in order to decorate the place. Every item was chosen to make the inn feel authentic and homey. She wanted people staying to feel as if they were guests of her great-great-grandparents who'd built the mansion so many years ago.

He tucked the papers back into his bag and crossed his arms. "Actually there's a lot wrong. Most places with as many rooms as we have enjoy a higher percentage of return customers and usually book their rooms to capacity for the five tourist-heavy months of the year. I've been over the records Ida kept that I found in the piles of paper in the office, and the West Oaks Inn hasn't been able to do that. Something has to change."

Here it came—he was going to fire her.

But he just breathed, heavily. Like a horse after a hard run.

He was going to destroy her ancestral home. She had to do something. She had to fight.

Maggie paced. "Part of the beauty of Goose Harbor is that we don't do things in a business-first way. That's why people want to visit this town. To enjoy a community that isn't focused on getting ahead and climbing the next ladder."

"Yes. But when business isn't thought of at all, our revenue stream suffers."

"Is that all you care about? Money?"

He made a face as if he'd bitten into something sour. "I'm the last person to want to amass wealth, believe me. But yes, I do want to be able to leave a legacy for my girls. I want to be able to send them to college and pay for their weddings without it being a huge struggle." His voice rose. Not in a yelling way, but it filled with passion. "I don't want to keep the inn looking old-fashioned. One of the reasons I left home originally was that I was sick of people telling me how to live my life. Well, I didn't listen to them then and I'm sure not going to listen to you now."

He studied the grass for a moment before making eye contact again. "My research has shown that people don't want to stay at their grandma's house—they either want high-end pampering or a place that's family-friendly. West Oaks isn't either."

"You can't do this."

"I can. And I will." He lowered his voice, stepping closer. "How can I make you see that this is a good idea?"

"You won't." She shook her head. "I'll never agree with you."

He sighed. "I would have liked you on my team, Maggie. But I don't need you on board with this. Now, if you'll excuse me, I have a designer to meet with."

And he stalked off across the yard.

Chapter Eight

The computer chair creaked as Kellen leaned back to re-read the two advertisements he'd written. Maggie wouldn't like either of them, but it wasn't up to her—was it? She was still angry with him for hiring a designer, but Sandra Conner had already sent over some great ideas. If only he could show them to Maggie and get her opinion instead of deciding on his own.

He leaned forward, bracing his elbows on the ancient desk. What if he did care about what Maggie thought? She'd never agree with him anyway. No matter how much he wanted her to. Women not agreeing with him was becoming the norm.

First Cynthia, who wouldn't see reason and refused to support his decision to leave the band and start anew, and now Maggie doggedly fighting him every time he thought he was making the correct choice regarding the inn. What he wouldn't give for someone—anyone—willing to stand beside him and promise to be there for the long haul. Be on a journey with him, instead of fighting him at every pass. Tell him his ideas and dreams weren't worthless or doomed to fail.

Kellen raked his fingers through his hair, pulling at the tips.

Perhaps that was his punishment for messing up so greatly in his past. Had he followed his parents' instructions from the get-go like his brothers, would he be happily married now? He definitely wouldn't have his girls.

But that was where he always got stuck—his daughters. As much as he regretted his past—his sins—he couldn't find it within himself to regret having his girls. And he never would.

Soon after becoming a Christian, Kellen had talked with his father about the subject, and his dad had reminded him that God was in the redemption business. In fact, he'd said that God would delight in redeeming the worst parts of him.

God had already redeemed his sin of being intimate before marriage through the lives of his girls. But what about the other parts of Kellen's soul? Would God ever redeem his passion for music or was that meant to be a sacrifice— forever laid down for the sake of walking with the Lord? If that was the price, Kellen would pay it. Willingly. He already had done so. And if that was what God wanted, Kellen would leave his love of music on the ground along with his desire for a family for his girls like the one he grew up in. After everything, he didn't deserve a wife. His past sins would cost his daughters a mother forever.

That was something he'd have to learn to live with.

A shadow passed across his computer screen. He swiveled in the chair to see who had walked by the open office door.

Maggie stood in the doorway with a plate in one hand and a large cup in the other. She offered him a small, friendly smile, and although she'd pulled back her curls in a low ponytail, a few strands had worked their way loose to frame her face.

In the past week he'd stopped seeing her hair as wild and unruly. It fit her personality perfectly. *Carefree.* The word had not struck him as positive until recently. Before, carefree had been his band members shirking responsibilities.

When it came to Maggie, she was exactly who she appeared to be. If she was angry with him, Kellen knew it. If she was enjoying herself, she wore her joy for everyone to see. If she was worried, there was no way to miss it. She threw herself into her tasks yet knew when to cut loose and declare it was time for a dance party in the kitchen with the girls. She didn't seem to care if someone thought she was being silly or strange. So many of the women he'd known in LA were concerned with what everyone thought of everything they did. Maggie wasn't like that. It was refreshing. Not to mention a great influence on his girls.

"Evening." He nodded.

"I thought you might be hungry." She lifted the plate, indicating it was for him. "The girls and I tried a few new recipes and they wanted to eat. We tried to wait for you."

"I know." He let his head drop against the back of the chair. "You were in here twice telling me to come to dinner and I kept working. I should have stopped what I was doing."

Maggie tentatively crossed the room and handed him the plate. She'd stacked enough food to feed two grown men. Heat wafted from two perfectly browned pork chops. They were covered in a cream sauce that smelled of garlic. Beside the pork chops was a large scoop of a warm casserole. Spinach, chicken and gooey cheese. The rest of the plate was taken over by three large biscuits. Kellen breathed deeply. She'd made the biscuits once before. They had cheddar folded into the batter and rivaled the ones served at most seafood restaurants. Correction: not rivaled—they were better.

"Wow. Thank you." He laid the plate on the desk and fought the urge to dive into eating right away. "What all do we have here?"

"Just some pork chops with a little different seasoning than I usually use, and this is a chicken Florentine casserole that I tried for the first time. You'll have to let me know what you think. I'm on the fence about it." She handed him the cup she'd been holding on to.

He glanced down at the liquid. Sun tea, probably mint. She'd made some a few days ago and he'd told her how much he liked it.

"Thank you." Kellen swallowed hard. "If it tastes half as good as it smells, then these recipes are keepers."

No one had ever taken care of him before or thought to look out for him. With his being the youngest, it had always been him doing things for his brothers. Then with Cynthia it had been about what she could gain by being attached to him. His daughters being so young, it was Kellen who had to think of how to meet their needs on his own.

"That's sweet to say, but you worked at a five-star restaurant. I'm sure you're used to the best."

"Everything you've made is ten times better than what we served there. Restaurant food isn't all it's cracked up to be."

"If you say so. Well, I'm going to tidy up the kitchen. I let the girls borrow my video camera and they're making a movie dancing to their favorite songs. My women's small group meets tonight, so I'm going to head out in about a half hour. Just make sure to lock up if you guys head to the cottage before I get home." Maggie turned to leave.

Did Maggie ever sit down and relax? She probably couldn't after managing the place on her own for so long. At least he could ease her load a little. Who stopped to take care of Maggie? No one whom he'd seen so far. But Kellen could.

In fact, he would tell her his idea now. That way she'd know going forward that she wouldn't have to shoulder everything alone anymore.

"Maggie, wait. I wanted to talk with you."

"Weren't we talking already?"

"I mean about more than food. About the inn."

"Oh." She bit her lip and studied the floor.

"I just emailed an ad to run in the newspaper this weekend. I'm going to hire someone else to help around here." He smiled at her, waiting to watch the relief wash over her features.

Her head snapped up, eyes narrowed. "Are you trying to get rid of me?"

"What?" He rocked forward in the chair. "No. Why would you think—"

She crossed her arms. "You don't think I do a good job here? What needs to be done differently? If you tell me what you want me to focus on, I can just—"

"Maggie." Kellen was on his feet, crossing the room. He cupped his hands over her shoulders. "I'm trying to help you."

"I don't need help. I ran this place just fine before you came along." She ducked away from him and backed into the hallway. "Excuse me. I should go."

"Maggie." He called after her, but she had already charged up the hallway and closed her bedroom door.

Kellen grabbed the plate and cup and headed to the kitchen, where he could keep an eye on Skylar and Ruthy. He didn't feel like working anymore tonight. A moment later the front door eked open and then slammed closed. Maggie never used the front door, but of course she would tonight, since he was sitting in the room with the back door.

So much for attempting to help. He'd try not to make that mistake again.

* * *

Locking the combination on her bike lock, Maggie scanned the parking lot. Despite leaving the inn earlier than she'd planned to, it looked as though everyone had beaten her to the church.

She climbed the front steps, tracing her fingertips over the wooden railing. The setting sun's last light blazed against the white-painted building. Inside, the church still boasted a new car smell. Goose Harbor had lost the original building in a fire just before Maggie's twentieth birthday. Her friend Shelby Beck, who'd been injured in the fire as a young teenager, had recently championed to rebuild the church. They'd held an opening ceremony a month ago.

Unfortunately it hadn't been ready for Ida's funeral. Ida would have loved seeing the church made new.

Maggie hugged Ida's Bible to her chest.

Her dear old friend had reveled in God's making long-desired dreams come to pass. Ida always encouraged Maggie to hold out for God's best and promised that God had a plan for Maggie's life that would exceed her expectations. The elderly woman had been wrong on that point. Always positive, but Maggie had learned that could be a bad thing. Sometimes hope was dangerous because it ate at the soul like termites on an old home.

Instead of spending the past few years dreaming, Maggie should have been focused on being content in her circumstances. Or at least she should have been planning for a way out instead of trusting that God would work out a way to take care of her. Always trusting the best. A best that never came.

Kellen was set on hiring another person for the inn. No doubt it would be someone with actual experience running a business. Someone far more organized and qualified than Maggie. Oh, sure, he'd keep her around for another month or two. Let her train the new person. Then what? Send Maggie packing? She couldn't tell him she had no money and no place to go. Never that.

Downstairs, Maggie located the room she'd heard the small group would use to meet in. Shelby had painted it a calming mocha color and given it cream accents. Plush chairs set in a half circle made for an ideal sharing space.

Paige Beck spotted Maggie first and came running across the room. "I'm so happy to see you. It's been too long. For such a small town, you've been hard to find." Paige pulled her into a tight hug. For a petite woman, her blonde friend harbored a lot of strength.

It was strange, how Maggie and Paige had become best friends so quickly. Paige was married to Caleb Beck—one of Maggie's childhood friends. He had once been Maggie's brother-in-law when Sarah was still living. She was happy that Caleb had found love again, but sometimes— in the deep places she didn't often acknowledge—it hurt seeing them together. It made her ache for a future that was long out of her grasp.

Oh, sure, there had been Alan. But he hadn't really been a viable choice. She should have known that selling his paintings at the local art gallery and fairs wouldn't have kept him satisfied for long. Alan had dreamed of his own studio. People paying thousands for a single painting. Even if he'd started his own shop off the main square, he'd never have been able to achieve that. He tried for a few years, and one of his paintings even hung in a guest room at the inn, but his ambitions had been beyond Goose Harbor.

Maggie hugged her back. "It's so good to see you."

Truth be known, Maggie missed the days when Paige had lived at the inn. It had been for only the first half of a school year, but Paige quickly became a sister to her.

Jenna caught her eye and patted a seat beside her. "I saved this one for you."

Maggie knew most of the women in attendance. Paige had brought along Bree and Amy, both also teachers at Goose Harbor High School. Maggie didn't know them well, but they'd always been polite. Everyone milled near a table that held cookies and drinks, catching up on life. But Maggie held back.

They would ask how she'd been since Ida passed away. They thought she owned the inn, so none of the women would have an inkling of Maggie's constant panic about losing it. No one would be able to understand the torment she felt in regards to the new owner. Sure, Maggie worried about the day that Kellen would tell someone he was the new owner and word would get out around town. But it hadn't happened yet. The second it did, Maggie would start getting calls and questions from people. Really, she should tell her friends before that happened.

What if they peppered her with questions about Kellen and she didn't know how to answer them? Kellen confused her. One minute she was butting heads with him and moments later she felt drawn to his kind and helpful spirit.

Sometimes Maggie believed that, as Ida had always promised, everything would work out for the best—including Kellen owning the West Oaks Inn. But then the rational side of her took over and knew for certain that nothing good would come of it. Kellen wanted change, and getting rid of her might be one of his "needed improvements" down the line.

Shelby Beck, Caleb's younger sister, made her way to the front of the room. "If you all can find an open seat, I'm going to get us started tonight. Thank you for coming. I'm so happy to see you all here for our first meeting. I think everyone knows each other besides Kendall." Shelby offered a wide smile to a woman with long chocolate hair sitting in one of the front seats. "She's new in town, so make sure to say hi to her afterwards."

Years ago, Shelby had been burned in the fire that totaled the original church in Goose Harbor. She'd spent many years since then covering the scars on her arms, back and legs. But lately, since she'd started dating fireman Joel Palermo, Shelby hadn't seemed so worried about letting people see her scars. Tonight she wore capri pants, kitten heels and a sleeveless top. It wasn't that warm outside, but perhaps she was making up for so many years of hiding. Maggie never understood why Shelby had thought that people wouldn't still care about her or want to be around her if they knew about the scars. The burns hadn't changed who Shelby was.

"I have one update before I put in our video for today." Shelby took a deep breath. "You all are the first I'm telling this to, but we're in our last stages of interviewing candidates for the position of pastor. We should be making a selection within the next week or two. Okay, now on to the video." Shelby pushed a button on the remote she held and then walked to the back of the room to shut off the lights.

The woman speaking on the video lesson talked about the importance of letting God build a home within their hearts. That the earth and things of the world would all pass, but God and the eternal things would remain. Might as well call the message *Maggie, Give It Up About the Inn Already*.

Maggie ripped her napkin into strips and piled the pieces on her empty plate.

Shelby flipped the lights back on and carried a Bible with her to the front of the room. "That was really challenging to hear, wasn't it? While she was speaking, a verse kept coming to my mind and I'm going to share it with you."

The pages on her Bible crinkled. "Here we go. Romans 5:5, 'And hope does not put us to shame, because—'"

"Sometimes it does." The words came out so quickly and automatically, Maggie had no time to cover them. Heat raced its way across her cheeks.

Shelby set down her Bible, her eyebrows diving. "Do you have something you want to talk through, Maggie?"

"No. I'm sorry. It's okay."

Jenna grabbed Maggie's hand. "She's right. I know it's not the popular opinion, but more often than not I've found that hope does put us to shame. There are things I hoped… dreamed…" Jenna shook her head and looked away.

Maggie slowly made eye contact with each woman in the room. Could she trust them with the truth? They would find out eventually. Better to hear it from her now.

Would they think she was a failure? Maggie was easily five years older than the next oldest person in the room. She should have her life together—the way they all seemed to. Well, besides Jenna, but Jenna was young. She had time to work through any issues. Whereas life was quickly passing Maggie by.

Maggie took a fortifying breath. "I may lose the inn. Well, honestly, I already have."

Paige tilted her head. "What do you mean? Is it money—"

She had to get the information out all at once or else she'd lose all her courage. "I haven't owned the mansion in years." She had to launch ahead before the questions started. "After my mother and grandmother passed away, there wasn't much money left over. I'd made some poor choices with some of it." If she could take back Alan, she would. She'd never waste a minute on him, let alone money. "And my mother's experimental treatments had drained us of most of the savings before that. It's expensive to manage a house that size. I loved my old job at the diner, but I couldn't handle the mansion's bills."

Paige leaned over and took her other hand, giving it an encouraging squeeze.

"There were so many medical bills even after my mother's death. Then there were maintenance things that hadn't been done to the house in a long time. I ran through most of the money just with upkeep. Do you know how much it costs to heat that place?" She shuffled her feet. "Anyway, I got to the point of needing to sell my home but was having a hard time coming to terms with leaving the house that's been passed down in my family all these years."

"Understandably." Jenna's smile was soft and sad. Her father's orchard had been in the Crest family for a long time, too. Jenna got it.

"Ida Ashby found out and offered to buy the place. We did it without telling anyone besides her lawyer, and Ida paid for everything after that."

Someone gasped.

Maggie plunged ahead. "Ida let me live there and manage it. She let people believe it was mine. But I have no claim to it."

Shelby dropped down to sit on the floor near Maggie's feet. "She didn't leave it to you in her will?"

Maggie shook her head. "She left it to her nephew Kellen Ashby. He's living in her cottage and he can get rid of me at any time." She took a deep breath. "I don't have much in my savings, I'm afraid. I was stupid. I never thought about the future and kept donating my money, thinking that was what God would want me to do, since I didn't have many expenses. Now I have nowhere to go." She shifted. "I'm so angry with God, you know? I've always done everything right. When other people were having fun I stayed back to take care of my family. When other people were dating, I chose to be responsible. But what has that gotten me? Nothing. I'm alone. I have no home. No money." Her voice broke.

"You have us." Shelby placed her hand on Maggie's knee.

"Thanks." Maggie shrugged, feeling restless. She'd taken her friendships for granted along the way, too, hadn't she? She made eye contact with each woman and saw the truth—she could have shared all of this with them years ago and they would have shared her burden with her. "That means a lot. You have no idea. But I still have to face losing everything. I'm so sick of hoping for a different story for my life, you know?"

Paige let go of her hand to offer a side hug. "I wish you would have spoken up a long time ago, but thank you for telling us now." She sat back but made sure she held Maggie's gaze. "If you need a place to live, Caleb and I have a spare bedroom. It's yours anytime you want it for however long you need it. You know he considers you his sister and won't mind if you crash with us."

"My apartment is only a studio, but you're welcome to squeeze in, too." Shelby smiled. "I'd love a roommate."

"Now, now, Shelby." Maggie laughed, trying to lighten the mood. "You'll be getting married soon and that'll be roommate enough, I think."

Shelby blushed. "We're not engaged. Joel and I haven't even been together that long."

The night dissolved into chitchat from there. On Maggie's way out of the church, Jenna caught up to her.

"Thank you for being brave and sharing all that." Jenna fell into step beside her.

Maggie laid Ida's Bible in the basket on her bicycle and entered the combination on her lock. "I don't know why I hid it for so long."

"We hide things because of shame. Even if it's not our fault. I know I do."

"I'm glad you're back in Goose Harbor." Maggie walked the bike to the street.

Jenna pursed her lips. "I'm learning to be glad about it. But hey, that's not why I followed you out. When you get home do me a favor and do an online search for Kellen Ashby, okay?"

"Okay."

Glad for the old-time lamps that lit the streets at night, Maggie headed home. The notes of a guitar met her as she bumped up the uneven driveway. Kellen and his girls sat out on the front porch of the cottage singing together.

It was Kellen's voice that cut through the still night air and worked its way into her heart.

"Lord, I want to know You. More so every day. To trust You, resting in Your promises. I know in Your hands I'll be okay."

Did she believe the words they were singing?

"Maggie!" Skylar's voice broke the song. "Dad says we have to go to bed. Can I have a good-night hug?"

"Sure thing." She might have a beef with Kellen, but she wouldn't take it out on Skylar and Ruthy.

The girls trotted across the yard, meeting her halfway. They wrapped their arms around her waist, making it impossible to keep walking. Maggie leaned down and pressed a kiss on the top of each of their heads.

"Would you tuck me in?" Ruthy whispered. The sweet longing in her voice broke Maggie's heart.

"I will, sweetheart. As long as it's okay with your father."

"Of course it's okay." Kellen stood two feet away, hands in his pockets and a guitar slung across his back. Looking like a model for a CD cover.

They all headed into the cottage. Skylar and Ruthy buzzed around the small rooms like happy little bees as they brushed their teeth and had *one more* glass of water. The kittens, Pete and Repeat, pranced around her feet no matter where she walked. She finally scooped up the little black kitten—Pete—and carried him into the girls' bedroom. Maggie helped tucked Skylar and Ruthy into their beds and then Kellen offered her his hand so they could all pray together. Maggie left Pete cuddled next to Skylar on her pillow.

Afterward, Maggie made a beeline for the front door as she and Kellen left the girls' bedroom.

"Wait up." Kellen caught her arm. "Are you all right, Maggie?"

If she'd been honest with her girlfriends, she could start being honest with him, too. After tucking in Skylar and Ruthy and praying together, she felt so safe and wanted. Perhaps that was the problem when it came to the Ashbys.

Unable to meet his eyes, she looked up at the ceiling. "I don't think I can ever help you put them to bed again."

He lifted his eyebrows in a welcome gesture, inviting her to continue.

"It hurts too much." Maggie clutched at the fabric near her heart. "I've always wanted this. Children, a hus—family. And I can't have it. That hurts."

In the narrow hallway, Kellen stepped forward and cupped her elbows. "Why can't you have it?"

Afraid to speak, she shook her head.

"You'd make a loving mother and be the best wife a man could imagine having. Don't ever give up hope, Maggie." He pulled her into a hug. "God has amazing things planned for you. I know it," he whispered close to her ear.

Taken by surprise, Maggie stiffened for a moment, but then relaxed. She'd been so young when her father passed away and had therefore spent her life hugging only women. When women hugged, it was like being enveloped in warmth. Even the fit ones had softness to them.

Hugging a man was entirely different. Maggie wrapped her hands around Kellen and pressed her palms into his back. He was solid and steady. His heartbeat close to her ear. For a minute, it felt as though she could hand over all her troubles to him and he'd be able to shoulder them.

If only he wasn't part of her troubles.

She pushed out of his hold. "Well, have a good night."

He followed her to the front door and stood in the doorway as she made her way across the yard. Would things be awkward between them now?

Back in the inn, she got ready for bed. Going through her usual routine, she checked all the locks and turned off all the lights. A glimmer from the office caught her attention and she checked to see what it was. Kellen had left the computer on.

She grinned and lowered herself into the computer chair. Shaking the mouse brought the computer screen back to life with a search engine open. Hadn't Jenna told her to look Kellen up online? Why not?

Maggie typed in his name and pressed Enter.

Instantly thousands of results came up. Pictures of Kellen walking on a red carpet. Photos of him onstage with a microphone in his hand. He had been some big deal in the music world. Snaggletooth Lions? She'd never heard of the band, but then again, Maggie only listened to her local Christian station, and from the look of the concerts in the images, Kellen's band hadn't been the praise-and-worship sort.

She clicked on an image to make it bigger. Kellen grinned in a three-piece suit, and a size-zero Barbie hung on his arm.

Was that Cynthia? A bio caught her eye and she gasped. He was almost six years younger than Maggie was.

Catching her hand halfway up to fix her hair, Maggie froze. What must Kellen think of her? Plain Jane Maggie, who hardly ever wore makeup, didn't own a pair of heels and had no clue how to tame her curls. Only minutes ago she'd clung to him like a lifeline. She'd even imagined herself fitting in to their ready-made family. *Foolish.* Kellen could never care for someone like her when he had shared the company of Hollywood's finest.

Maggie hit the minimize button and retreated to her bedroom. He'd told her he managed a restaurant. Had that all been a lie? More important—how long would he actually stay in Goose Harbor? Based on the pictures she'd just viewed, Kellen could never be happy staying in Goose Harbor long term. Not if he was used to a life of glitz and glamor. Goose Harbor would become boring for him and he'd have to leave eventually. Just like Alan.

A guy used to models on his arm couldn't make a life here. He had to be fixing up the inn in order to sell it.

She was about to lose her home for good.

Surprisingly the thought of Kellen leaving suddenly bothered her more.

Chapter Nine

"Yes. It'll be completely doable to merge the two remodeling plans and go with a modern, yet family-friendly one." Sandra bustled past Kellen in the inn's upstairs hallway, furiously typing away on the tablet that forever rested in her hand. Did the sophisticated designer ever put the contraption down? She didn't seem the type.

One more reason Kellen preferred Maggie to any other woman. Maggie didn't even own a smartphone. Let alone a tablet or any sort of technology that she carried around with her at all times. While doing so would probably bode better for the inn, he wouldn't ask her to change that about her personality. Not when it was a trait he found so attractive.

Kellen glanced out the rounded windows in the sitting area on the second level. Maggie worked out in the front yard, cultivating one of her many gardens. Every now and then she'd rock back on her feet and joke around with Skylar and Ruthy, who were playing nearby. Tending things came easily to Maggie, whether it was plants or people's spirits. She was gifted at caring and seeing needs.

He'd stopped wondering if she had manipulated his aunt after their first trip to the beach together. No, he couldn't believe that about her now. In fact, Maggie wasn't trying to get on his good side at all, and that was what she'd be focused on if she wanted to use him.

Kellen rubbed his hand over his mouth, hiding a chuckle. The woman showed no fear when she wanted to go toe-to-toe with him about something. While he would welcome her support, it was comforting to know Maggie wasn't going to smile and say yes to everything he said in order to get something from him.

They hadn't revisited their talk after tucking the girls in the other night, but the conversation had played over and over every day in Kellen's mind. Maggie *would* make a great mother and wife. Any man worth his salt could see that. Why hadn't a man noticed those qualities in Maggie yet and shown her she was worth being cherished and pursued? If only he could turn back the clock, Kellen could have been a better man in his youth.

He could have been worthy of her.

If he made a move—would she accept him? He ran his hand down his face, blowing out air.

Probably not after she found out about his days with the Snaggletooth Lions, and he'd have to come clean at some point.

"Okay." Sandra still looked down at her tablet. "Let's run over a few of the changes that we're sure about. Follow me."

Kellen allowed himself one last glance out the window at the three females visiting and laughing together. Just maybe Maggie could accept him as is. He'd told her to hope. Was it time to follow his own advice?

After signing the tablet for Sandra and scheduling a time to start the demo, he spent the rest of the day in his office calling guests and rescheduling some of them. Noise from the kitchen made it hard to hear some of his phone conversations. At some point during the day, Maggie and his girls had stopped gardening and had moved to making a ruckus in the kitchen.

Kellen swiveled in his chair. He needed to accommodate the eight-week period of construction that Sandra said it would take to transform the interior of the inn. The outside would remain the same for now. He'd consider expanding only if the inn launched well.

Once the construction crew knocked down a few walls upstairs, there would be fewer guest rooms, but each room would be larger and the upgrades would mean he could charge more. Heated bathroom floors in all rooms, two rooms would now boast full kitchens, and a grand suite with all the trimmings would be the crowning piece of the West Oaks Inn. They'd call it a honeymoon suite and charge a bit more. People bought in to that sort of thing.

Skylar tromped past his office on her way back to the kitchen.

"Hey, Sky, want to help me color on some walls?" He scooped up a few fat permanent markers and made his way to the kitchen. The girls would get a kick out of being allowed to draw on the walls the construction crews were going to remove.

Sitting on the island counter, Ruthy grinned at him while she stirred what looked like chocolate-chip cookie dough. "We're making something special, Daddy."

"I can see that."

Flour powdered the counter and spilled onto the floor. There were little footprints from Skylar stepping in the stuff and running around the island. Ruthy snagged a handful of chocolate chips and popped them into her mouth.

"Looks like you missed a spot." Kellen crossed the kitchen and dragged his finger through the flour. He dotted it on Ruthy's nose. "Ah. There. Perfect."

Skylar bounded forward, wrapping her arms around his legs. "Get me, too, Dad!"

"Oh, you, too, huh?" He dusted his hands together, making it snow flour down onto her.

She squealed and darted around him.

"Oh, you can't get away that easily." Kellen stuck his hands back in the flour piles again and advanced after Skylar. She dashed behind Maggie. Tugging on Maggie, Skylar used her as a human shield.

Resting her hands on Skylar's arms, which were snug around her waist, Maggie surveyed the disaster in the kitchen as if she were seeing it for the first time. "I'm really sorry about this mess, Kellen. I know you like things more organized and orderly."

"I don't mind." He stalked forward and pointed at Skylar, who had peeked out from behind Maggie.

Skylar screamed and ducked behind her again. "Save me, Maggie!"

"I'm surprised." Maggie leaned to block the giggling girl. "Because not all that long ago this sort of thing used to bother you a lot."

He shrugged, coming closer. "It doesn't anymore. I'm learning to enjoy moments like these. That's something you taught me." Then he tossed his voice so Skylar knew he was talking to her. "You can't hide there forever."

"I can."

"Or I could just go after Maggie. What do you think, girls?" He waved his floured hands.

Maggie's eyes grew wide. "You wouldn't."

Kellen lifted his eyebrows. "Oh, wouldn't I?"

"Get her, Daddy!" Ruthy drummed her feet against the cabinets.

Maggie shrieked as he advanced. She brought her arms up to block her face, but he grabbed her wrists and pulled her snug against his chest. Skylar made a break for it, but he already had his victim. Maggie's wide smile let him know her struggling wasn't real. He breathed deeply— Skylar had been right; Maggie always smelled like cinnamon. Which made Kellen remember his mother's cooking growing up. Maggie smelled like home. He leaned closer, their foreheads almost touching. *Kiss her.*

Maggie lightly pushed against his chest and he let her go, smearing flour all over her forearms in the process.

Her eyes went wide. "Kellen Ashby!"

"That's my name."

She dusted off her arms as she tried to hide the obvious grin tugging at the corner of her lips. "If I knew your middle name I'd use it right now."

"Wyatt. But don't tell anyone." He went back for more flour and then dotted her nose and both cheeks. He made a big show of stepping back to assess his work as his daughters giggled behind them. "Huh. I should have become an artist. You're a masterpiece, if I do say so myself."

Maggie grabbed a dish towel and swatted him. "Funny. I thought musicians were considered artists."

Kellen froze.

The good mood he'd been in disappeared quickly like a crowd at an outdoor venue during a sudden rainstorm. How long had she known? Since the beginning? After everything, was he still such a bad judge of character? He'd never be able to trust his read on people again. If Maggie had been aware the whole time, why hadn't she mentioned it before now?

Shoulder muscles going stiff, he turned his back to Maggie and flipped the handle for the faucet. Shoving his hands under the ice-cold water, he let the sensation break through his thoughts so he could form words.

Kellen gripped the edge of the sink and closed his eyes. "How long have you known?"

"Oh, about your band? Only since last Thursday. Sorry I didn't recognize you before—I'm not up to speed with what's current in music."

Last Thursday.

Kellen did the math in his head.

Right, that would be the day she'd all but confessed to him that she wanted to be part of his family. An uncomfortable feeling sliced through his gut. *Betrayal.* She'd used him. Played him just like Cynthia. But worse, his girls were involved. And more than he cared to admit, his heart had been involved, too. Hadn't he almost just kissed her?

He pressed on the bridge of his nose. "Sky, Ruthy, it's time to head home."

"It's still early…"

"But the cookies…"

"No buts. We're going home." Kellen moved to scoop Ruthy up off the counter while still keeping his back to Maggie.

Maggie put her hand on his arm. "Did I say something wrong?"

"Actually—" he grabbed the door handle and started to leave "—you said exactly what I needed to hear."

No use waiting for a response. With Ruthy snug in one arm he took Skylar's hand in the other and headed back home. There would be no more evening hangout sessions with Maggie going forward.

If Maggie had been worried about losing her position before, with the new girl starting today, it felt almost certain. Kellen had backpedaled on his idea to hire someone else to help her cook and clean, but then insisted that they needed someone business savvy to plan events, help with marketing and handle their social media.

Maggie waved goodbye to the couple from Ohio who had spent the past five days at the West Oaks Inn. They were down to only two serviceable rooms since Kellen and his girls had drawn all over the walls in the other ones. Not that the rooms had all been booked for the week, but still. No one else was scheduled until the reopening happened after the remodel. A reopening that the new girl would plan.

How would Maggie make it through the remodeling?

She went through the motions, tugging the sheets off the guest bed and taking out the trash. But even doing normal chores felt pointless. In the coming days she'd have to pack up all the items in the rooms and they'd move out the furniture to make way for the impending changes. Kellen hadn't even shown her the new floor plans. Not that she wanted to see them. Seeing them might make the fact that the innards of the home she grew up in and loved were about to be pulled out, thrown away and completely forgotten. While Ida had kept most of the home intact, the construction permits Kellen plastered to the front window told her he would not.

She made her way down to the kitchen. As she filled the sink, Kellen breezed in the back door.

"Morning." Elbow deep in suds, she tossed the word over her shoulder.

Kellen nodded once and made a half-grunt greeting sound and continued walking. It had been the way with him for a little more than a week. Since the flour fight. He'd been acting…standoffish.

"Check's on the counter," he finally called from the office.

Sure enough, in a sealed envelope with her name printed

on the front she found a paycheck. It was far more money than Ida had ever handed to her. If she could continue working for the next few months she could build up a nest egg. She'd be able to leave, find a local job cooking and rent an apartment close to town. Printed on the left-hand side of the check was West Oaks Inn Inc. He must have snuck off to the bank at some point and set up a business account. So the knowledge that he owned the place and not Maggie would start circulating.

Maggie had no clue how Ida had run everything. So relieved that Ida had saved the West Mansion, Maggie never considered questioning her on business practices.

How had Maggie ever thought she could run this place? She had a hard time saving money even without expenses. Not that she was wasteful—she tried not to be. For the first time Maggie realized she probably couldn't have run the inn well if she had been given the reins. The realization hurt.

Asking Kellen whom he had told about the inn was out of the question. Not with his current grumpy mood.

Was he offended that Maggie hadn't known about the Snaggletooth Lions? If so, the man needed to learn to get over himself. His near miss at stardom didn't impress her one bit. Probably used to girls fawning over him. Not her…well, not any longer. She hadn't fawned per se, but she'd started hoping. And hoping was far more dangerous than fawning.

Since first looking him up online, she'd poked around on the internet some more. Curious. He'd led the band on a path to stardom but dropped out a week before a record deal was signed. The songs played on the radio didn't include him singing, but he had written all of them. Maggie printed out the lyrics and read them over. While not sung in a way she liked—far too loud—the content and subject matters covered in the songs were deep. Saying goodbye to a terminally ill loved one. Battling self-doubt. Struggling with loving someone who didn't love back. Letting listeners know their lives mattered.

She'd also gotten ahold of the songs from the band's second album. One Kellen had nothing to do with. The songs had lost their punch. They were about partying, finding the best girl at a club and a man covering his tracks after committing adultery. She'd stopped reading lyrics after that. In the reviews she'd located, music critics panned the second album and most cited the loss of their songwriter and front man as the missing piece.

The doorbell sounded and Kellen left his office to get it. Being nosy, Maggie stepped into the doorway between the kitchen and the public part of the inn. The girl at the door couldn't have been more than twenty-two or twenty-three years old. Tiny in stature, with dark hair accented by red lowlights, and she had it pulled back in a stylish clipped bun. The woman wore dress pants and a formfitting white button-down, looking as if she were arriving at an accounting firm for work. Not an inn.

"Right on time." Kellen smiled down at the woman. A huge, Hollywood-worthy, handsome smile.

Maggie crossed her arms, shoving her fisted hands under her biceps.

The woman handed him a shiny portfolio and followed him inside. Maggie watched her assess the inn. Her eyes went to the grand piano situated off to the right of the lobby. Next, her gaze bounced to the large crystal chandelier that lit the dining room. Maggie's great-grandfather had purchased the huge piece as an anniversary gift, supposedly telling his wife that as bright as it made the mansion was as bright as she made his life.

Kellen cleared his throat. "Annika Graft, this is Maggie West. She also works here."

"Oh." Annika laid her hand on Kellen's arm. "I go by Nika. Always Nika."

Who touched their employer like that on their first day on the job?

The huge grandfather clock in the parlor sounded for the half hour.

Summoning a smile, Maggie reached out to shake her hand. "Nice to meet you."

"You, too." Nika beamed at her. "I've driven past this place so many times and wondered what it looked like inside. It's exciting to now be a part of it. I mean, look at this railing." Nika crossed the room and ran her fingers over the intricately carved wood.

Kellen pressed his hand over the top of the portfolio. "That's actually not staying."

Maggie spun to face him. "You can't take that out. It's original with the home. It's part of the appeal. It…" Was a part of one of her favorite memories.

"Sorry." He shrugged. "It doesn't fit with the new aesthetic."

Together they gave Nika a tour of the mansion and Maggie discovered it was impossible not to like her. She oohed and aahed at the right moments, tripped adorably when there was nothing under her feet and sounded genuinely thrilled to be at the West Oaks Inn.

Kellen ended the tour in his office. "This is where you'll be spending a lot of your time. Just like we talked about in the interview, you'll spearhead our social-media presence, and I need your organizing expertise." He shook the mouse, waking up the computer. He glanced over his shoulder, looking right at Nika. "You know QuickBooks?"

"Of course." She stepped closer. Too close.

Maggie hung back as they launched into a discussion on the wonders of financial software. Nika dropped into the chair and immediately started showing Kellen a few ways to streamline the inn's cash flow and spending accounts. Kellen had one hand braced on the arm of the computer chair and the other on the desk, leaning near Nika. Of course, he'd have to in order to share the computer screen. But an angry clawing feeling worked its way through Maggie's stomach.

The look on Nika's face bothered her the most. Whenever she'd tip her head back to make eye contact with Kellen, Nika had the expression of a girl meeting a crown prince. Open. Hopeful. How did Kellen inspire that sort of adoration so quickly?

Maggie shuffled back in the room, rubbing her arms.

Perhaps that was why she and Kellen couldn't get along. Maggie had never approached him the way Nika was doing. Maggie had fought with him, challenged him and treated him the same as she would anyone.

Okay. The last part wasn't entirely true. Maybe when she first met him it had been, but as she got to know him, she'd started to care. Kellen and his daughters had worked their way quickly into a place in her heart that she'd thought she'd shut down long ago. Family. Home. Even the hope of being loved someday had returned.

They still hadn't acknowledged that she was in the room with them, so Maggie bowed out and headed to the back door, toward her gardens. She'd work on the far edge of the property today. Down near the mill.

Newly opened flowers gently bobbed in the spring air, filling the yard with their sweet perfume. She'd always loved gardening because it made sense. If she followed a care-and-maintenance schedule, they'd produce and flourish 99 percent of the time.

The same philosophy hadn't rung true in Maggie's life. She'd been the well-behaved kid in class, the daughter who caused her parents no stress and the girl in the group who let her friends speak up because it was kind to let them have their way, right? Saying what she wanted over them would have been selfish. And if she'd been anything, it had been the model follower of God growing up in her church. She hadn't dated in high school, because she'd valued purity and never broken the rules. When her sister moved on, it was Maggie who hung back to assume household responsibilities and care for ailing relatives.

All of her life she'd spent carefully doing everything right—for what?

Wasn't God supposed to bless those who made their choices in a biblical way? Who obeyed and put others first?

If that was the case…how come everyone else got their dream and Maggie was left holding fistfuls of dirt? Alone. Again.

Maggie shoved on her gardening gloves and found a secluded area near the river and began to weed. She tugged on a large dandelion. But it wouldn't budge. She tugged again. Still nothing.

She rocked back on her heels and swiped the back of her arm over her forehead.

How could she have believed there was a future for her with Kellen? So foolish and immature. Like a teenager falling for a photo of a guy in one of the trendy magazines her sister, Sarah, used to hoard under her bed. But Kellen had been open with her and kind and he'd sought out moments to spend time together in the evening. Yet she'd read all that wrong.

He'd never been interested in her. More than likely, it was convenient to make Maggie feel as if he cared so she'd watch his daughters at a moment's notice. A man like him probably just used her to pass the time until someone better came along. Someone like beautiful, young, organized Nika.

Chapter Ten

After wrapping the final vase in newspaper, Maggie lowered it into a packing box. She dusted off her hands and stood. Spinning once, she took in the almost barren room and sighed.

She could do this. At least, she'd have to.

Besides, putting the decorations in storage until Kellen decided what he wanted to do with them—that she could handle. While she enjoyed all the antiquing adventures she'd gone on to locate each of the pieces in the inn, it was the structure she cared about. Not the possessions inside.

Downstairs the tinkling bells let her know that someone walked in through the front door. Maggie stretched. Probably Nika, although both she and Kellen had instructed the younger woman to use the side door going forward. Without expecting guests, they should just lock the front from now on. Although, come to think of it, Nika wasn't expected today. She had a family function to attend.

Kellen? He rarely used the front door, either. It could be a walk-in guest, hoping to book a room. They really needed to hang a notice near the West Oaks Inn sign that announced they were closed for construction. Even if part of the upstairs wasn't going to be touched, Kellen and Maggie had decided not to subject potential guests to all the dust and noise that would evidently come with the remodel.

Maggie hustled down the hallway and took the steps two at a time.

An older woman wearing a gentle smile waited in the lobby with an old-style carpetbag clutched in her hands. She had long white-silver hair and a soft, motherly figure.

"Hi there. I'm afraid we can't accommodate guests right now due to construction." Maggie offered her hand. "However, I can recommend another bed-and-breakfast close to downtown that has the same feel as this one if you'd like."

The lady scrunched her brow as she worked her pursed lips back and forth. "That won't do for me. I really wanted to stay here and my cab's already left."

"I'm so sorry." Maggie patted her hand.

She set down her bag. "Is my son around? Maybe he has room."

"Your…son?"

"Kellen."

Maggie felt her eyes go wide. "Mrs. Ashby. I'm sorry. Follow me. I didn't know we were expecting you. Right through here." She stumbled over her own feet as she led the way to the kitchen.

Mrs. Ashby grabbed ahold of her arm, righting her with a stronger grip than Maggie would have guessed she had. "Now, dear, as I understand it, you're usually not one to lose your head, so don't do so on my account."

"You know who I am?" Maggie couldn't hide the note of disbelief that colored her voice.

"Maggie West. Am I right?" Kellen's mom left her bag on the kitchen table and pulled out a seat. "I knew it was you the moment I saw you. It's like I've known you for years."

Needing something in her hands, Maggie opened the

fridge and pulled out a pitcher of sun tea. Ever since learning Kellen loved the stuff, she'd made a new batch every couple days. "Tea?"

"Mint. Right?" Mrs. Ashby winked. "That's Kellen's favorite."

"I'll let him know you're here." Maggie reached for her phone.

Mrs. Ashby waved her hand, dismissing the need. "He can wait. Right now I want to visit with you."

Maggie set a cup in front of Kellen's mother and then lowered herself into a chair on the opposite side of the table. "Mrs. Ashby, I have to ask. How do you know me?"

"Call me Susan." She took a long swig of the tea. "That's the best sun tea I've ever tasted. Kellen was right about your kitchen skills."

"He's talked to you about me?"

She nodded twice in an exaggerated manner. "Ida, too. Like I said, I've known you—been praying for you—for years."

What did Susan know? While it made Maggie slightly uncomfortable realizing that Susan had heard stories about her—enough that she felt as if they were friends already—that feeling was quickly overrun as the second statement sank in. *Been praying for you for years.*

"You...you prayed for me?"

"Pray-*ing*. That *i-n-g* on the end makes it an action verb. I believe God calls us to action and that's an everyday sort of thing. Don't you agree?"

Maggie folded her hands together on the table then flipped them over, examining the lines on her palms. "Honestly? I haven't been speaking much with God lately. Don't get me wrong, I'm a Christian, but I have a lot of unanswered questions right now."

Kellen's mother was younger than Ida by a good ten to

fifteen years, but the conversation felt just like their old talks. Growing up with her grandmother, mother and sister, Maggie found it easier to open up to a woman than to speak to a man about…anything. The recent situation with Kellen proved how terrible she was at understanding the male species.

Susan reached across the table to cup her hand over Maggie's. "One thing you must understand is that as long as we're breathing oxygen on this earth, there will always be unanswered questions. That's where the trust and hope parts of the Bible come into play."

"Hope," Maggie whispered. "I don't even know if I have it in me to hope anymore."

"I've got extra. You can borrow some of mine."

Maggie shifted in her seat. "Thanks. But it's still not my favorite word these days."

With her hand still covering Maggie's, Kellen's mom bowed her head for a few moments. When she lifted her head again, she waited to speak until she had Maggie's eye contact. "You have been good and faithful and God sees that. Don't believe the lie that He doesn't or that your obedience didn't matter. All right? Because that's the furthest from the truth you'll ever get. Truth is, God treasures you and has kept you safe."

"How…?" Maggie breathed the word.

"Like I said." Susan squeezed her hand tight and then released it, sitting back in her chair. "I know you and have been praying for you for a very long time. Action, Maggie. I want you to remember that. Our Lord believes in verbs. We don't need to speak in past tense, because good or bad, our past doesn't matter at any given moment. What matters is today. Are you more like Jesus this afternoon than you were this morning? That's how we should all be thinking."

"What about the passages in the Bible that tell us to wait?"

"Oh, my dear, waiting *is* action. Don't you go believing otherwise."

Her words worked like a balm, seeping into the hurting parts of Maggie's heart. If what she said was true, then Maggie's obedience hadn't been a waste. Moreover, Susan was right. If Maggie loved God as she said she did, then it should show in her everyday life. Being a Christian wasn't summed up by knowing a date of conversion. No. Like Kellen's mom had pointed out, it was a daily walk, a minute-by-minute conscious effort of growing closer to God.

Maggie sucked in a long, shaky breath. "Thinking back, I've made myself a little cocoon inside the walls of this old house. I'm safe, but I'm also closed off. Far away from everything. It's kept me protected. Maybe too protected."

Susan offered a tender smile. "Time to come out, little butterfly."

The side door opened and Kellen stopped with his hand on the knob, an instant of shock that quickly turned into joy. A huge, goofy grin broke out across his face. "Mom!" He rounded the table in four steps and enveloped the older woman in a tight hug. "What are you doing here? I wasn't expecting you. Is everything all right?"

His mother kissed both his cheeks and then cradled his face in her hands. "Do I need a reason to see my youngest boy?"

He kept grinning.

"Now." She rose slowly. "Let me see those grandbabies."

"I was only coming to grab the mail real quick, but that can wait. Let's load you into the car and we can go pick up Ruthy from the sitter now, and then later we'll get Skylar when school's over. They'll be so surprised." Kellen wrapped his arm around his mother's waist. Susan looked older than Maggie would have expected Kellen's mom to be. Then again, he had three older brothers and she had no clue as to the age difference between all the Ashby siblings.

"Hang on." Susan pressed her hand over Kellen's chest. "I have something for Maggie." She reached into the folds of her large coat and pulled out a wrinkled envelope. "For you, dear."

"I don't understand." Maggie took the envelope, staring down at the aged paper.

"Perhaps it'll hold some of those answers you're looking for." Susan winked and then left with Kellen.

Maggie locked the side door behind them and then went and locked the front door. Alone. Gripping the envelope on her way up the stairs, she wondered what she'd find inside. She climbed into the window seat, leaning her back against one of the arched windows. Then she drew her knees up as she opened the envelope. A breath locked in her chest; she unfolded the piece of paper inside. A letter.

Magpie

"Ida," Maggie whispered. She didn't need to glance down to the signature to know her old friend had written the note. The only person who called her Magpie had been Ida.

Well, now, if you're reading this, then I'm dancing with my Henry again and I'm spending time at the Lord's side. That's a good and happy thing, Magpie. I hope you know that. I've been loved greatly twice in my time on earth—by Henry, but more than anything, by God. I'm truly home now.

You have a question for me, though, so I thought it best to try to offer you an explanation. Namely, why did I leave the West Oaks Inn to Kellen and not to you? Oh, go on and pretend you weren't concerned about that, but I know you—that old home is eating you up and tying you down like a staked dog in a small backyard. Don't tell me it isn't.

My heart aches for Kellen. He was the youngest with three highly achieving brothers and was often overlooked. From a young age he was told that the thing he wanted to pursue most—music—was sinful. Can you imagine how confusing that would be? Being told that something you're gifted in and have a passion for displeased God. He should have been encouraged to pursue his dream in a way that shone a light on the Gospel. But he wasn't and he ran.

Kellen is not without mistakes, mind you. No, he went and made some of the largest ones a man can. But in the end, he chose correctly. He gave up everything for the good of his daughters and has sacrificed his dream in the process. I respect him for that and when I got word by his mother that Kellen never got to see his girls working that job in Los Angeles that he didn't much like to begin with, well, I knew I had to do something about it.

You must understand that he's my nephew and he has two small lives depending on him. Moreover, that man deserves a happy ending and I believe with all my heart that he'll find that in Goose Harbor. Much like I did after Henry passed through my friendship with you, my dear.

Might I be honest with you? You are wonderful at many, many things, but you're not the best at managing money and are not organized. Putting the inn in your hands would have been dropping a large and cruel burden on your shoulders. The money it takes to run this place! In order to take care of it I would

*have had to leave you every cent I had left, and that
would have meant turning my back on Kellen. And
I couldn't do that.*

*I trust that Kellen will take care of you as I did.
More than that, I believe you two have the opportunity to take care of each other for life. You do understand my meaning? I know it is scary for you—this
man you do not know now has power over the one
thing you hold tightest. Might an old friend offer one
last piece of advice? Let go of old ideas and dreams
in order to make way for new ones. I pray both you
and Kellen learn to see the beautiful picture God's
been painting before you for years. That will only
happen if you start trusting it will, though.*
Much love as always,
Ida Ashby

Maggie ran her thumbs back and forth over the wrinkled paper. It hit her how much she still missed Ida, but the
woman wouldn't have wanted her to mourn. She was glad
to have the letter, even just for one last item to hold on to.
Then again…hadn't Ida warned her about that?

Sadly Maggie had been holding so tightly to the old
West Mansion that her hands weren't free to cling to Jesus.
That didn't sound like the obedience she prided herself in
at all. She'd been wrong to feel as though she deserved
life to work out better for her than others simply because
she'd followed some correct algorithm that others hadn't.
More like she'd followed a set of rules instead of following in the footsteps of her savior. *Ouch.*

So much to think through.

Did Ida's letter, along with some personal revelations
that she'd had while speaking with Susan, mean that Maggie should pack up and leave the inn? If Ida's heart had

been to take care of Kellen and his daughters, then they should get to live in the private portion of the mansion. It was far bigger than the cottage was. Much more room than Maggie needed. That would solve her situation with Kellen.

Paige and Caleb had contacted her over the weekend, letting her know they were serious about offering her a place in their home for a while. If she moved in with them, though, it would still be temporary. She couldn't stay with her married friends forever. It wouldn't be home.

Maggie scanned the letter again and fought a smile. Ida seemed to be trying to play matchmaker from the grave. Too bad. She was wrong on that account. She and Kellen weren't about to take care of each other for life. Even if the idea sounded like the best new dream Maggie could have imagined.

Kellen parked his car and strained his eyes. That was Maggie all right. But why was she army-crawling across the grass with Skylar? Looping his arm over the steering wheel, he watched the pair of comrades.

Kellen's ears still stung from the multiple tongue-lashings his mom had given him since she showed up at the inn three days ago. As usual, his mom was right. Annoyingly so. He'd judged Maggie based on his past experiences instead of treating her like an individual. Kellen didn't know her motives, and while he needed to protect himself and his daughters from people who might wish to use them all in some way, Maggie's other actions had shown that her aim wasn't to use him. In fact, everything pointed to the opposite.

She deserved an apology. Again.

The sun's rays blasted into his closed car, heating the inside where he sat despite the day only being mild. He watched his daughter and Maggie whispering together near the wildflower garden. She was really good with his girls. Which was a plus.

Kellen shook his head.

Maggie was an employee. Someone who performed a job at the inn—end of story. *What if it's the beginning of the story?* No. No way. No how. Kellen was damaged goods. Maggie deserved better than someone like him. His thoughts kept heading in that direction because his mom kept mentioning the possibility. Had told him they were a match and that his aunt Ida had prayed for them to end up together.

That was all.

Skylar and Maggie bolted up from the ground and then, hand in hand, raced into the house. Their laughter followed them like a soft boat wake. Kellen climbed out of his car and crossed the yard to the inn, walking carefully, so as not to make noise. He heard a bee buzzing nearby and picked up his pace. Taking the stairs two at a time, he eased the door open quietly. They hadn't spotted him yet. Ducking along the wall, he spied the two playing in Maggie's family room.

"Okay. This couch is the fire truck and you get to be the fire-truck dog," Skylar instructed.

"The dog? Are you sure? Couldn't there be a firewoman on the truck?"

Skylar shook her head solemnly.

"You can't say I didn't try." Maggie laughed and put her "paws" up in the air. She pretended to pant like a dog. Kellen had to bite his tongue to keep from laughing.

"Oh no! Maggie-dog! There is a fire. C'mon, grab the hose." Skylar tossed her a pillow and they both sprang into action, pretending to put out the fire on the other couch.

Skylar dropped the cushion to pop her hands to her hips.

"Now the couch is a pirate ship. I am the pirate and you are a prisoner. I'm going to feed you to the sea monster, so you have to walk the plank."

Kellen considered breaking in to tell Skylar she was acting too bossy but decided not to. Watching Maggie play so willingly with his daughter when she had nothing to gain by doing so caused a warm feeling to work its way into his heart.

Maggie shimmied onto the armrest and Skylar poked her in the back, every inch of his daughter playing the most menacing of pirates.

"Please! Captain Skylar Blackbeard, please spare me."

"Nope. Walk the plank." Skylar nudged Maggie again until she threw herself onto the floor, flailing her arms in the air, sputtering and all-out pretending to drown.

Finally Kellen stepped into the room and broke out in a deep belly laugh. Maggie froze.

"Daddy, you are the sea monster and you have to eat Maggie."

Kellen stepped so he had a foot on either side of Maggie, looked down at her and winked. "Aw, we don't want to eat Maggie." He prodded her with his foot and in a stage whisper said, "You're supposed to still be drowning."

"You have to eat her, Daddy. That's part of the game. It's what sea monsters do." Skylar crossed her arms.

"What if I get to save Maggie instead? I'll be another pirate and take her on board my ship. How about that?" Skylar still looked skeptical. "I mean, Sky—we like Maggie, right? We probably shouldn't eat her, even if it's by a pretend sea monster."

Skylar closed her eyes for a second, scrunching her eyelids so her face bunched up—a telltale sign that the child was thinking really hard. The grandfather clock in the lobby sounded.

"Okay, Dad. You can save her. But your ship has to be outside on the hammock. You don't get to be by my ship."

Kellen wasted no time reaching down and scooping Maggie up. He tossed her over his shoulder and strode toward the door in the kitchen as she pounded on his back lightly with her fists.

Maggie laughed. "All right. We get the picture. You can put me down now."

"Hey. No complaints. I'm saving you. It was this or be eaten, remember?"

Her hand stilled against his back. Skylar darted around them, holding open the door. Kellen walked the ten paces out of the house to where a hammock hung under a large cotton tree.

"Our ship awaits, fair maiden." He tossed her down, falling himself in the momentum.

They were both laughing until their eyes met. Only inches away from her, he instinctively traced his gaze down her face to her mouth. What was she thinking? In a second he could close his lips over hers. Would she let him? He wanted to, which surprised him. Would his feelings for this woman ever make sense? Could he trust her, completely, the way he wanted to?

A little voice broke into his thoughts. "Now you have to kiss her. That's what a hero does when he saves the girl. They do in all the movies."

Maggie became rigid beside him. Kellen leaned back on his elbows and cleared his throat.

"Where's your grandma and your sister?"

Maggie rolled over and crawled out of the hammock. "They went for a walk. Skylar stayed here to help me make some bread."

"From scratch." Skylar jumped onto the hammock with him, sending it swaying dangerously. "Hey, there's Grandma."

She pointed toward the sidewalk. His mom had Ruthy by the hand, and clutched tightly to her chest, Ruthy had a bouquet of wildflowers. Skylar jumped off the hammock and ran toward them.

"I better check the bread." Maggie pointed her thumb over her shoulder, in the direction of the inn.

"Hey, Maggie." Kellen clambered down off the hammock and caught up with her. "We need to talk."

Maggie spun around, her cheeks flushing. "I'm sorry I didn't recognize you. Pop culture isn't really my thing. If it bothered you so much, you should have just said something from the beginning and then I could have—"

"I'm glad you didn't know."

"But this whole past week…" She didn't need to finish the sentence for him to understand. He knew how he'd been acting.

Aloof. Unsociable. Rude.

"I'm trying to apologize for how I've been behaving. It had nothing to do with you and everything to do with me." He scanned her face. Creamy skin that never needed makeup, the palest blue eyes and her auburn hair, Maggie was gorgeous. How had he missed that before?

"Ah." Maggie clucked her tongue. "Going with the old 'it's not you, it's me' line."

He had to make her see he was being genuine.

Kellen hooked his hand on the back of his neck. "I hate when people know about my past. I'd rather no one recognized me from the Snaggletooth Lions. The person who played in that band isn't me. Not anymore. I'd rather just be known for who I am now."

Maggie crossed her arms, assessing him. "And who is that man? Because I keep getting mixed signals."

"He's a father who adores his two little girls." Kellen

pointed toward his daughters and mother as they made their way up the driveway. "A struggling businessman." He moved his hand to indicate the inn. "And someone who is trying to figure out how to live a life that pleases God, but I'm still failing all the time on that account." He laid his hand over his heart.

"You and me both." Maggie blew out a stream of air that ruffled her hair. He fought the desire to reach up and tuck the wayward strands behind her ear.

"You? Now, that I don't believe." Kellen stepped closer, lowering his voice as his daughters drew near. He picked up Maggie's hand, cradling it in his. "You're the kindest, most caring, most self-sacrificing person I know."

She looked down at their hands. "I'm so confused. I've been questioning everything about myself lately."

He tightened his hold. "Come with me to the Sandy Point Bridge tomorrow morning."

A smile tugged at the corner of her month. "How early in the morning?"

"Early." He traced his thumb back and forth over her smooth skin. "Watch the sunrise with me."

Little footsteps pounded closer. "Daddy, I got these flowers for you."

Maggie extracted her hand. "The sun doesn't rise over Lake Michigan. It sets."

"The sun still rises." He smiled, hoping they could go back to their easy friendship. "Say you'll come with me."

"I'll think about it. But for now, I need to go grab that bread before it burns."

Maggie headed off and Kellen turned to hug his girls. He'd put a bug in his mom's ear about the bridge. Since Mom was staying in one of Maggie's spare rooms, she'd have plenty of time to bother Maggie until she gave in.

Not his most noble move, but he wanted some time alone with Maggie and he'd do what he had to in order to get it.

Chapter Eleven

Maggie buckled her seat belt and cradled the blanket on her lap. Kellen climbed into the driver's seat and closed the door. Darkness enveloped them until he flipped the headlights on.

Susan had pestered her, saying she would watch the girls, until Maggie had texted Kellen, saying she'd join him in the morning. True to her word, Susan had been cooking when they left and had two pajama-clad girls serving as assistants. Even though the cottage had brand-new appliances, Kellen and his family often used the kitchen in the inn to make their meals, seeing as the one in the cottage was so small.

"This is early, even by my standards." Maggie stifled a yawn. "And I'm used to getting up before people to make multiple courses for breakfast."

"You'll live. Promise." He nudged his elbow against hers on the center console.

Purple hints of twilight snuck through the canopy of towering trees as he maneuvered the car out onto the main highway. Sandy Point Bridge would be a thirty-minute drive. A pedestrian bridge in the midst of the forest preserve, it took a fifteen-minute hike to reach it from the parking lot once they got there. Childhood memories told Maggie that the time investment would be worth it. There was something special about the spot. The bridge connected a divide between dunes in the preserve, hanging above a wide river connecting to Lake Michigan. The cold lake water meeting the river caused a thick layer of fog to grow under the bridge every morning—making it look as if it were floating in the clouds if someone had the imagination to pretend away the trees nearby.

After parking, Kellen clicked on a flashlight. "Want me to carry the blanket?"

"I've got it." The coarse fabric scratched against her bare arms.

The hike was entirely uphill. Kellen offered his hand as they clambered over downed trees and huge roots sticking out of the ground. Birds tittered on the higher branches. Whether they were disturbed by their morning visitors or were simply planning their flights for the day, only the birds would ever know. Something darted on the ground, rustling bushes. Stifling a scream, Maggie dug her nails into Kellen's arm.

"Killer squirrels." His laugh was soft, comforting.

She swatted his arm and trudged on ahead of him.

Both of them stopped walking when the bridge came into view. Long, slender fingers of pink blushes and purple lights traced over the sky, lighting the opening to Lake Michigan. Despite being warm from the walk, Maggie shivered as air blew off the lake and whistled through the gap in the dunes. The bridge, while not overly huge or tall, was breathtaking. Only suspended for pedestrian use, it was narrow and dipped into the fog that laced through the ravine.

Maggie could hear the river below but couldn't see it through the thick haze.

She smoothed out the blanket and dropped to her knees, sitting back on her heels. "This is truly one of the most beautiful things I've ever seen."

Kellen lowered himself close to her. She could feel the fabric of his sleeve as it touched her arm. *Take his hand.* She shook the thought away.

He didn't take his eyes off her. "It sure is."

Maggie grabbed his chin and pointed at the floating bridge. "That. You goofball."

They sat with a cloak of awed silence wrapped around them for a few minutes. Maggie watched Kellen out of the side of her vision. He seemed deep in thought; perhaps she should be, too. She glanced back at the bridge. The top of the fog reached the bottom boards and flowed over them like a rising flood.

Wanting to break the silence, Maggie sighed. "You know, most of the time I feel like that bridge probably does."

"What do you mean?"

"As beautiful as it is right now, it's all alone. It's completely surrounded by that fog. From its perspective, it has no idea what's all around it." Maggie drew up her knees, wrapping her arms around them. "For all that bridge knows, Godzilla could be waiting under it in that fog, or a cannon could be aimed right at it, ready to destroy the bridge completely. The bridge is completely clueless because of the fog. My life is a lot like that."

Kellen half smiled at her. "If you really think there might be a giant lizard huddling in the small space under the bridge, then I'm sorry I didn't bring my camera."

There was probably enough room for a giant bear or two to hide in the fog, but definitely not a city-destroying lizard. It was funny to think about it just the same.

Maggie yanked her phone from her back pocket and gave it a triumphant pump in the air. "Behold. The power of the camera phone. It may not be a smartphone, but this puppy still can snap a picture if it has to. That scaly monster won't be able to get too far away before I can take a million pictures of him with this." She winked at Kellen, who wore a goofy grin as he watched her. "I'll sell the photos for millions and then we'll build a cabin and live happily there forever on our Godzilla riches." A huge smile tugged on Maggie's lips. She used to have a quick wit that never failed to make her sister or Caleb laugh. It had been too long since she felt safe enough to be silly. She'd figured a woman her age was past that. But Kellen's chuckles made her believe that joking might be a lifelong thing.

"Will *we*, now?" Kellen emphasized the *we*. "Okay, now that we have the Godzilla plan finalized, what's this about you feeling alone?"

The sun had crept onto the horizon since they arrived, slicing rays into the fog.

She laced her fingers together and stared at them for a moment. "Maybe *alone* isn't the right word." She shrugged, struggling to make him understand. "I mean, Goose Harbor is a tight-knit place. Everyone knows of me, but no one knows me. I hope that makes sense. And I have friends—some really amazing ones—but there is a divide. I'm probably explaining this wrong. So not alone, but more like separate or different."

"Separate and different... Is that such a bad thing?"

"It is when the different part means you're thirty-five and don't have a husband or a future mapped out." Had she just blurted her age to him? Heat crept up her neck. Not that he probably hadn't figured out that she was older, but now she'd confirmed it for him. Too late to take it back now, she pressed forward. "Or when you're separate because everyone has moved on in life, leaving you in the same place you were when they left ten or more years ago."

Kellen scrubbed his hand over his chin. "You mentioned a man by the name of Alan before."

He'd listened closely. She'd mentioned Alan only once.

"Ah yes." Maggie rocked forward a bit. "What is there to say about him? Alan was the 'don't worry about it, babe,' starving-artist type. Pursing his dream of painting was his number one drive. I should have seen it at the time, but I think at that point I was so desperate to be in a relationship—any relationship—that I settled below my standards."

Kellen dropped his hand to the blanket. "Do you care if I ask what those standards are?"

"Does it even matter anymore? I've long given up on a Prince Charming coming along, so I tossed the list out years ago."

"But you remember some of the list, don't you?"

"Strong morals. Christian background. When I was young I dreamed of being my husband's first kiss." She laughed once, but the sound held no humor.

Kellen's Adam's apple bobbed.

"Alan spent more time and effort honing his craft than actually speaking to me. He'd come to me when he needed to bum some money. You know, because working a nine-to-five gig messed with his muse. Some hogwash along those lines."

"Gotcha." Kellen rolled his eyes. "He was one of *those* artists."

"And then some." Maggie pushed up from the ground. "My friends warned me about him, but I didn't listen. It's funny how much you can lie to yourself in an effort to protect your heart."

She paced to the edge of the bridge. Most of the fog had rolled away and she could see the river. "I should have seen it coming, but I didn't. Alan grew tired of Goose Harbor. He said it didn't stimulate his mind enough. I made the mistake of loaning him most of my savings." *Or all.* "He told me if I loved him I shouldn't have qualms about doing it. He promised to come back for me. You can see how that worked out."

Kellen growled. "Tell me he gave you back your money."

Maggie shook her head. "Last I heard he'd made it to New York. I tried to track him down. I sent letters to his mother's home in Virginia hoping she'd forward them, but they were never answered. I even filed a police report, but the investigators said they couldn't help me, since a crime wasn't committed. I could have gone after him in a civil trial, but that would have cost more money that I didn't have."

"Could you go after him now?"

"I'm over it and I still don't know where he is. Besides, I never recovered financially." She swallowed hard. *Say it. Tell him. Kellen cares. Right?* Even if he didn't care, maybe he'd be less inclined to cut her from the inn's staff when the chance came. "I feel like a loser admitting this to you, but I have almost no money to my name. There were medical expenses for my mom that needed paying, and those two things wiped me out. Ida only gave me what I needed."

Her back to Kellen, she heard him shift—rising—and take a few steps. Beside her, still looking down at where the river met the lake, he laced his fingers through hers and gave her hand a pump. They stood like that, palm to palm, for a few minutes.

"I'm sorry that happened to you," he whispered.

"It was so long ago." She pursed her lips. "It's nothing."

"But it is." He tugged on her arm lightly, turning her to face him. "Love should never be used as a weapon. Not as a tool to manipulate someone."

His eyes searched hers, silently asking questions she didn't know the answers to.

Maggie pivoted so they were shoulder to shoulder again. In a hoarse voice she hardly recognized, she whispered, "I don't know what I'm doing with my life anymore. I might not have ever really known. Everyone my age is married and starting families. If not that, then they have successful careers. What do I have? Nothing. I have a job at an inn that I could lose at any moment."

"You have that job for as long as you want it."

"Thank you." She took a shuddering breath and brushed her hair away from her face. "This is probably a much heavier conversation than you were hoping to have this morning."

"This is perfect." He turned her toward him again and placed both of his hands on her shoulders. Maggie hooked her hands over his biceps. The guitarist had been hiding his muscles.

He locked gazes with her. "I want to know you, Maggie. If you haven't noticed, I have trouble trusting people and believing the best about them. You make me want to do that, though. It took me a while to get over my past, but I'm here. I believe the best about you."

She licked her lips. What should she say to that? *I believe the best about you, too.* But did she? Last night she'd stumbled on more internet articles about Kellen. Rumors of him dating a string bean of a woman only months ago. Another one about an A-list starlet who regularly commented about the fact that he was her dream man.

The look in Kellen's eyes said he wanted to be with Maggie. That he cared about her. In fact, if her feminine radar was working correctly today, she'd guess Kellen was a few encouraging words away from kissing her. Did she want that? *Yes. No. Maybe?* How many women had he kissed? She wouldn't compare to what he was used to.

Removing a hand from her shoulder, he used it to tip up her chin. "Do you feel any better after saying that stuff?"

"I still feel very surrounded by that fog." His nearness was far too exhilarating. Maggie took a step back, breaking contact. She rubbed her forehead. "A little lost and unsure about my surroundings and future."

"Maybe you're seeing the fog the wrong way."

"Meaning?"

"What if it's not fog at all? What if it's a cloud of grace?" He slipped his hands into his coat pockets. "You know what? I think you're exactly where you're supposed to be and there is nothing wrong with not knowing what's next. There's a lot right about it, actually. Maybe those people with detailed plans are the wrong ones. See, you're leaving room for God to work. And maybe—just maybe— God's protecting you with that cloud instead of keeping things from you."

His words warmed her heart. She fought the desire to turn toward him because she really wanted to wrap him in a tight hug. To feel his chest rise and fall with breath against her cheek as she slipped her hands under his coat. As Ida had written, Kellen Ashby might have made mistakes in the past, but he was a man after God's own heart now. And today was what mattered. She should have trusted him. Should have let him kiss her. Now the moment was gone.

"A cloud of grace." She propped her hands on her hips. "Huh. Thanks. I like that."

"It's yours, free of charge." His smile was soft, welcoming. "Seriously, Maggie, you're safe in God's arms. You know that, right? There's no better place to be and there is nothing wrong with being different than everyone else."

It struck her that a few years ago, when she'd still been clinging to a list of ideals in a future husband, she would have written off Kellen instantly. Not that she was sure he was husband material at the moment, either, but he wouldn't have gotten a second thought. Mentally she pretended to toss all her old ideas down into the river. Feeling lighter, she gathered up the blanket and extended a hand to Kellen. He took it and didn't let go until they were safely back at the car.

Chapter Twelve

"You're happy." Kellen's mom nudged him in the ribs as she leaned around him to clean off the counter. They'd decided to make French toast in the cottage that morning instead of invading the kitchen at the inn.

"Why do you say that?"

She stopped and held his face in her hands. "I hear you humming, whistling and singing. You've never been able to keep those melodies down when you were in a good mood. They just spill right out."

Head cocked, he rubbed his palm against the side of his neck. "I hadn't noticed."

"Well, I sure have. And I know why you're singing again." She turned back around to the counter.

Stepping closer, Kellen caught his mom in a tight hug before she could conquer the rest of the crumbs. "I'm glad you came. Thank you for being here. The girls love having you around. I do, too."

"I love you. I have for every minute since I knew I was going to have you." Her voice sounded as though she might start crying.

Tightening his hold, he started humming an old children's song she'd taught him when he was in their church's kids' choir. Funny how the tune came back to him after it had been buried for so long. The lyrics talked about God having His hand on the sheep and how God cared about the one sheep that wandered and saved it from falling in the valley.

Replace sheep with Kellen and the cute little Bible song about summed up his life.

He'd turned his back on his parents for years. No communication. No trips home for Christmas. His stubborn pride had cost him so many memories. Not anymore. "I was thinking, for this Christmas and Thanksgiving, too, if I can swing it with stuff at the inn, maybe the girls and I can come to Arizona and spend the holidays with you and Dad."

"You know I'd love that, but what about Maggie?"

Ah. So Mom had picked up on the glances that he and Maggie shared across the dinner table many times in the past week. Or the way she turned to smile at him first whenever one of his daughters said something funny. When he was younger, he'd thought his mother possessed superhero powers because she'd been able to read all her sons like sheets of music. Perhaps that came with being a mom.

Kellen set his mother back so he could see her face. "What about her?"

"Well." His mom wrung out her dishrag and then attacked the counters in the cottage's kitchen again. "I wouldn't want you leaving Maggie all alone, so if you're coming you'll have to bring her along, too. Which would mean turning down guests at peak times, of course."

"Ma…"

"Although she may insist on staying here with how tied she is to that place and all." She tossed the rag into the sink and rinsed off her hands. "If that's the case and none of your brothers are planning to come home, then your father and I might just have to travel back up here and share Thanksgiving with you. But we won't be able to leave the church at Christmastime. Your dad will have to preach."

"There's nothing going on between me and Maggie."

"Of course there's not." She winked at him. "But I'm just saying that a lot can happen in seven months. A whole lot."

Speaking of the woman in question—Kellen strained his neck to look out the window on the far edge of the kitchen. The yard between the cottage and the inn was too wide; he couldn't spot her. Instead he pictured her spinning around in the kitchen, creating a mess while she prepared lunch. Even though they didn't have guests until after the renovation, she'd insisted on making most of the meals for him and the girls, and Kellen hadn't been about to turn down cooking as good as hers. Besides, the girls loved being Maggie's helpers and he enjoyed watching Maggie interact with Skylar and Ruthy. The three of them had quickly formed a tight bond.

Kellen swallowed hard.

As much as they loved their grandparents, the girls would probably revolt at Christmas if they didn't bring Maggie along.

His heart might, too.

"She's a good match for you." His mother's voice broke into his thoughts.

Once his mom got on a topic, she tended to act like a shark on a chum trail. He needed to redirect her or find a way to end the conversation before she started asking questions that he hadn't allowed himself to process.

"We should head over. Lunch is always on time." He tapped his watch.

He held the door open for his mother and then helped

her with the rusty gate latch, too. If it weren't for the fact that half the time there were strangers milling around on the inn's property, he'd have removed the fence between the homes by now.

A loud delivery truck reversed down Maggie's driveway. Kellen spotted Maggie on the front stoop, struggling to get her arms around the huge package. Picking up his pace, he jogged over to meet her.

"Here. I can get that." Kellen waved his hand, motioning for her not to bother with the delivery. Probably one of the items he'd ordered anyway.

"I'm okay." Maggie bent in a way that made Kellen nervous. If the package was as heavy as it looked, she'd throw out her back carrying it up the steps, across the porch and into the inn.

Kellen braced his hands on the top of the large box. "I know you're fine, but I'm still going to carry this in for you."

"I've *got* it." Maggie reached around him but then lost her footing and stumbled backward.

He caught her wrist, keeping her on her feet. His thumb rested on the place where her pulse pumped on the underside of her arm and he finally looked at her. Really looked. Red-rimmed eyes that were half-lidded. Hair more puffed out to the left than the right. Chapped skin near her nose.

"You're sick."

"Thanks?" She grimaced.

"Not— I mean, you're not feeling well?"

"I'll live." She coughed into the crook of her elbow.

How long had she been feeling sick? Why hadn't she called him?

He bit back his questions. "I'll grab the box. You get the doors."

"I'm strong enough to pick that up."

"I know that. One of the things I like about you is how capable you are."

"But…you said I was disorganized…" Her cheeks flushed. Fever?

"You *are* disorganized, but I'm not. We make a good team that way." He laughed. Kellen had been doing that more lately, hadn't he?

Finally relenting, she trudged to the front door and held it open as he lugged the box and heaved it up the stairs. She shouldn't have been trying to lift heavy things while she was sick. What could it be? The flu didn't usually strike in spring. A cold? Allergies?

His mom had let herself in through the side door while he and Maggie were bickering over the delivery. She opened the door to the private part of the inn and held it for both Maggie and Kellen. None of the normal smells he'd come to anticipate—baked goods, crisping bacon, fresh-cut flowers—met him in the kitchen. An empty pot sat on the counter beside a few bottles of spices and a wrinkled three-by-five card. Squeezing past the counter island, Kellen made his way to the office and left the box on the floor near the desk. He'd open it later.

Right now he had a stubborn woman to deal with.

So dizzy.

Maggie braced her hand on the table and looked down, focusing on the wood grains while she sucked in a sharp breath of air.

Her head pounded like an overcaffeinated woodpecker and her throat ached. She hadn't been able to sleep much the night before. Staying up until one in the morning to start packing the dining room more than likely hadn't helped her situation.

Footsteps brought her back to attention. Susan Ashby studied her from a few feet away.

"I'm so sorry." Maggie forced herself to focus on Susan's face even though her eyes wanted to close. "You're both probably hungry. I haven't even started lunch yet. I was trying——" She stumbled over to the card with her grandmother's recipe for baked-potato soup. "It shouldn't take long. I'll start now."

"No, you won't." Half-shadowed, Kellen loomed in the hallway with his arms crossed and his eyebrows drawn together.

"It's quick. I promise." She opened the refrigerator and pulled out heavy cream and the secret ingredient, hot sauce. When she turned, Kellen was right behind her. She bumped into him.

"Maggie." Kellen took the carton of cream from her slowly and set it on the counter, then did the same with the hot sauce. "Why don't you lie down and rest?"

"I can't. There's lunch to make and the lobby needs to be packed up and——"

He held up his hands. "And it'll all get done. But right now you need to relax."

"Don't you see?" Her voice took on a pleading quality. Didn't he understand? He'd said she had a job for as long as she wanted it—but that could have been just pity talk in the moment. She had to keep up with her daily tasks. More than that, she had to protect the history inside the West Oaks Inn. Yes, she was learning to let go of her hold on the place, but it was still her only tie to her family. She wanted to make sure her mother's prized antiques were securely packaged so they wouldn't break. Besides, she didn't like being still. "I've got things to do."

She tried to brush past him, but Kellen hooked an arm around her waist and pulled her snug against him. Maggie's hands landed on his chest, and her breath caught. He wore his cologne again. Fresh lemon mixed with an after-rain scent.

His gaze locked with hers. "Let me help you."

"I can't."

He let go of her, his shoulders slumped. "Someday, you'll have to let someone help you. Why not me?"

She shifted her gaze, studying the cuts on the counter-top. "It's just…I want to make sure it's done right. There's a trick to the soup and…"

"So tell me the trick." He turned her, guiding her toward the living room.

Maggie spotted Susan sitting at the table with a book and a smirk. Pretending she couldn't hear their exchange when she clearly could.

"But—" Maggie had no argument. She was tired. And it would be so nice to have a day to reenergize. Then again, that meant tomorrow's workload would be doubled. It never just went away.

Kellen had his hands on her shoulders, walking behind her as he steered her around the end table to the couch. She sat and pursed her lips. "But I—"

He held up a hand. "For someone who says that no one ever helps you and that you feel all alone, you sure turn down offers to help left and right." He grabbed a quilt from the back of a nearby chair.

"I don't."

"You do."

She closed her eyes, absorbing the thought. "Okay. I might be guilty of that."

His gentle chuckle washed over her. "Let someone take care of you. Trust me to do that." He tucked the blanket around her and then pressed a quick kiss to her forehead. "Rest, Maggie."

Her eyes shot open, but Kellen's face remained passive as he left the room. The kiss hadn't meant anything to him. A sweet gesture. Habit. Something he did when he tucked his daughters in every night. *Don't read into it.* But oh, it felt nice to be kissed and worried over.

Murmurs of conversation carried from the kitchen as well as the occasional spoon clanking against a pot. Bacon frying filled the air with a mouthwatering smell and the pinging sounds of grease dancing. It would taste amazing crumbled over the soup. A breeze from the open window behind the couch made the lace curtains sway.

Maggie leaned back on the cushions and closed her eyes.

She had been out only a few minutes when her phone buzzed in her pocket. Groggy, she pulled it out and tried to will her eyes to focus on the text from Paige.

Read Matthew 10:29-31

Pushing up from her cocoon, Maggie reached for Ida's Bible, which sat on the far end of the coffee table where she'd left it a few days ago. Untouched. She flipped it open, her eyes landing on the list of names written inside. She traced the line that she and Kellen shared. Why had Ida put their names together? There had been lines under that she could have used. Was there a reason or was it a mistake?

Shaking her head, she turned to the book of Matthew and located the verses Paige had told her to read.

Are not two sparrows sold for a penny? Yet not one of them will fall to the ground outside your Father's care. And even the very hairs of your head are all numbered. So don't be afraid; you are worth more than many sparrows.

Sparrows, huh? Paige knew her well enough to understand that she wouldn't be offended by the comparison. A sparrow was as ordinary and uninspiring as a bird could get. Their mousy-colored feathers made them blend in. No one considered them pretty. So unnoticed and small that they were often forgotten about. Yet God cared about every single one of their lives and was aware of what happened to each of them.

If the God of the universe cared about a little, ugly bird, how much more did He love her? She'd never been alone, had she? No. Not really. Even if it had felt that way at times. As Kellen had pointed out, she'd been stubborn. Even toward God. Trying to manage her life and assuming He wouldn't want to be a part of her daily struggles. Believing that He didn't see all she had on her plate.

God had wanted to help her all along. That she saw now. She'd complained loudly, but she'd never asked for help. The two were very different.

Forgive me. Don't let me be a birdbrain about this stuff again.

In the past two months, the dirt in her heart had been tilled by the girls in her small group, by Susan, but most of all, by Kellen. Buds were poking through the ground. Something new and fresh was happening. Maggie couldn't quite explain it, but she felt changed.

Kellen appeared in the doorway. "Feeling any better?"

"A lot, actually." She laid down the Bible.

He set a bowl of soup in front of her and went back to the kitchen for a cup of mint tea. "I realize these two don't normally pair together, but I was thinking—" His phone started to ring. Kellen fished it out of his pocket, and color drained from his cheeks when he looked at the screen. "I… One second."

Turning his back to her, he lowered his voice by a fraction. "Hello?"

Whoever was on the other line had his full attention.

Kellen slowly dropped so he was sitting on the coffee table, facing away from her.

"Really? No...this is great. Amazing. I'm just surprised." He hooked his hand around the back of his neck as he spoke. "I, uh, couldn't say right now. But...sorry, still in shock. Yes. That sounds fair. Talk to you then."

When he hung up, Kellen rested his elbows on his knees and stared at the phone.

Maggie sat up fully. She moved to put her hand on his back, but then let it drop. "Good news?"

He glanced at her over his shoulder. "I think so." His eyebrows were drawn together as he sighed. "I need to go. I have to—" He stood suddenly and paced away. "Don't worry about the mess in the kitchen. I'll take care of it later." He walked toward the kitchen. "Enjoy your soup."

Maggie stared at the doorway after he left. If it was good news, why didn't he seem happy? Construction was set to start on the inn tomorrow... Maybe it was only about that.

Chapter Thirteen

He had to go over and check on the remodeling. That was an owner's job, right?

Kellen shoved his hands in his pockets and entered the inn.

Contractors arrived by seven thirty in the morning every day for the past week. They'd blasted through walls and moved plumbing. Today they were updating electric and installing a few new tubs.

Nika ducked out of the private part of the inn. "Oh, it's just you." She'd finally given in to wearing jeans and T-shirts, dressing sensibly like Maggie always did.

"What are you working on today?" Kellen craned his head to see if he could spot Maggie in the kitchen.

"Social-media stuff. Do you want to see the banners I designed?"

"Later. I'm going to walk the house first." He ran his tongue along the back of his teeth. "Is Maggie around?" It felt as if she'd been avoiding him since the demolition of the rooms began.

"She was only here for a few minutes after I arrived. I have no clue where she went. Should I call her?"

"No, it's fine. I'll get ahold of her if I need to."

A fine layer of sawdust covered the wooden floors. He'd have them polished and refinished at the end. Make the place shine. The inn was morphing into something he could really be proud of. Maybe he'd change the name in the rebranding. A whole new image and new clientele. Finally a dream in his life that he could keep and call his own. One he didn't have to be ashamed of as he was about his past with the Snaggletooth Lions.

Holding tightly to the handrail, he took the stairs two at a time.

The landing was wider now. The hallway, too. But he'd kept the sitting area by the circle of beveled windows. Maggie told him it was her favorite spot, so he'd instructed Sandra to restore the area and fit it into the new design. Seven guest bedrooms had become five, but they were five that would demand a higher fee and stay booked during the high-travel season, which was quickly approaching. Nika would plan a successful grand-opening party and hopefully they'd have a great summer.

An image of him and Maggie strolling on the beach at sunset while holding hands sprouted in his mind. A great summer indeed.

Except he wasn't sure he'd be here in the summer.

Minor problem.

Kellen shook his head. He'd probably be here. Right? He'd yet to make up his mind about the offer he'd received from the Christian band Since Grace. Hadn't even told his mother. He needed to weigh the pros and cons on his own before he spoke to anyone about it. Processing was something he did alone.

He slowly walked through each room, inspecting new fixtures and imagining what each area would look like. The floor was ripped down to the plywood subfloor. They'd given him an estimate of six weeks to complete all the work and it looked as though they'd need every minute of that time to finish. Kellen would check in with the contractor later, but they were all on a lunch break or back at the hardware store at present.

Anyway, he hadn't come for the contractors. Not really.

He'd crossed the yard to see Maggie. Kellen had avoided her since the day he received the call from Since Grace's agent. But he missed her.

The lock that usually hung on the hidden door at the back of the hallway was off. Maggie told him once that the door led to the attic. Had one of the contractors removed it? There was no reason for them to be up there. If he held on to the inn, he might refinish the attic and use it for more rooms. These old Victorians usually enjoyed high ceilings at the top. He might as well see what the space looked like.

He climbed the ladderlike stairs. Sunlight bathed the crowded area, flooding through four rounded windows. Boxes and trunks were piled throughout the attic. Old belongings. Did anyone know this stuff was up here?

Someone sniffled.

"Hello?" He squinted, trying to find the person, but there were too many things blocking the way in the attic.

"Go away, Kellen."

"Maggie?" Stumbling over a few bags, he found her leaning against a pile of trunks with her feet against a wall. The wetness on her face made his stomach twist. He dropped to his knees beside her. "What's wrong?"

She rubbed her nose. "I'm so stupid. I thought I was ready to say goodbye, but I don't know if I'll ever be ready." She dropped her head into her hands, covering her face as more tears came.

Kellen sat down beside her and placed his hand on her back, rubbing small circles. "Goodbye to who?"

"Not who." She sat back suddenly, pinning his arm behind her. "The inn. This house."

He winced a bit but didn't say anything. Best not to upset an already worked-up woman. "The inn will still be here. It'll just be a little shinier. You'll see."

"No." She shook her head. "It'll be different. It already is. I saw them tear down the wall that used to be…" She rocked forward, biting her lip.

When she moved, he freed his arm. All his fingers started to tingle as blood returned to them. "You're right. It'll look different, but it'll still be a successful inn. I promise."

She leaned her head back against the dusty trunk and tipped her face to study the ceiling.

What was her issue? Why couldn't she be excited about the remodeling? Be on his team?

He swallowed hard. "Don't you trust me?" He might as well have asked her if she loved him. For him, they were one and the same.

She kept her gaze locked on the sharp nails that dotted the ceiling. "This used to be my home."

"It still is."

"No. Before it was an inn, it was my home."

"You owned the mansion?"

She let out a long stream of pent-up air. "It's been in my family for more than a hundred years. My great-great-grandfather built it for his wife. He said the size of the house needed to match how much he loved her. This was the biggest building on the shore for many years. The contractor tore through the wall in their old room today. It was…hard to watch."

The home was her final tie to her family and Kellen had torn it to pieces. Told her with a bold face he could do whatever he wanted with it.

"Maggie…I had no clue." His voice sounded small. "You should have told me before we started working."

"It's not like you care about the house. But me? It's been handed down for years. My parents left it to me and I lost it. Everything my ancestors worked for. Everything they left. It's all gone and it's my fault." She finally met his gaze. "You really didn't know it was my home?"

Unable to speak, he shook his head.

"The *West* Oaks Inn. My last name is West."

"I thought because it sat on the west end of town…"

"We're south of town. Not west."

"If I had known—" Then what? He wouldn't have handed over the inn. He couldn't now. The inn was his only source of income, especially if he turned down the other offer…

"I used to slide down the railing every morning to come to breakfast. Race my sister down. For a long time, before we converted it to an inn, one of the rooms smelled like my grandmother. After she was gone I'd lie on the floor and just breathe. The rooms upstairs hadn't changed in the first remodel. They were all I had left of my family. And now…" Fresh tears trailed down her cheeks.

What had he done?

He leaned his head back against the trunk. "I'm so sorry. You have no idea how sorry. I must look like a monster to you—tearing apart a place that holds so many memories."

"You're not a monster, just a man making his dreams come true. My dreams just happened to be in the way. You like to push forward and I like to cling to the past. I see that now. I just—" She laid her hand on his arm and pursed her lips together.

Past versus present. Did it always come down to that with Maggie?

Kellen took a deep breath and covered her hand with his. "Maybe it doesn't have to change so much. I'll show you the plans. We could rework it a bit to make you happy."

Her smile didn't reach her eyes. "You reminded me at the bridge that I need to learn to let go and trust what God's doing in my life. A cloud of grace, right? Maybe with all of this—the house changing and feeling like the last of my past is being ripped away—like you said, God's not doing something bad, but bringing about change that in the end will be for my good. I'm going to cling to that right now."

"But Ida remodeled the house. You were okay about that."

"It was a necessary evil then. It was only remodeled slightly so it didn't lose the house entirely. It still had the rooms I'd grown up in. Now they're gone—basically only this attic and the front part of the house are the same."

"I'm sorry. I don't know what else to say or how to make this better."

She sighed. "I'm going to go for a walk. I'd like to do so alone, if that's all right."

"Of course." *Don't go.*

Could any of the work be undone? Stopped?

She left, but she didn't go alone. Kellen's heart and his prayers went with her.

Kellen and his mom loaded the girls and a basketful of their favorite toys, movies and books into the car and headed to the north end of town, where the Rowes lived. Mrs. Rowe had invited his mother and the girls over for brunch.

Saturdays he usually reserved for time with his girls and now his mother, who was still visiting, but the conversation with Maggie the day before had him on edge.

He needed to convince her that they could make a compromise on the inn's remodeling.

Funny, in just under two months he'd gone from trying to find a way to get rid of Maggie to being willing to do anything not to lose her.

The houses in the Marina Lights subdivision were the biggest and most expensive in the area. Some were directly linked to the beach by long, zigzagging sets of stairs built against the dunes, and others were megamansions that sprawled all over their property. However, the grandeur didn't impress him. He knew all too well that money didn't solve problems. There was just as much pain behind the walls of mansions as anywhere else.

He glanced in his rearview mirror and smiled at Skylar and Ruthy. "What do you guys think of Maggie?"

"She's the nicest and best person in the world." Skylar bounced in her seat. "Well, besides you, Daddy."

"Thanks, Sky." He sent a wink to her by way of the mirror. "What do you think, Ruthy?"

She looked out the window, watching the little red lighthouse stand duty over the whitecaps breaking on Lake Michigan.

"I like when she hugs me. I pretend she's my mom and she loves me." Ruthy spoke so quietly, Kellen had to lean a bit over the console and crane his neck to hear her.

Her words hit him like a sucker punch. The muscles in his arms and shoulders flexed, shoving his back into the seat. Hard. For the past two years he'd tried to be everything for his daughters, but he'd never fit the role of mom. He could hug them a million times and offer to braid their hair, but that didn't replace a woman's influence in their life. They needed the compassion and understanding that only someone like a mom could offer. They needed Maggie.

His mother laid her hand on his arm and rubbed it gently.

Suddenly pursuing Maggie felt like too much pressure.

As if he were back in his father's church again. A boy being told how to sit and what to say and not say. He crumbled under that level of pressure last time around. Would he now when his girls were depending on him?

He wouldn't, because he had God with him this go-round, and because he'd been wrong about his father's church. They would have accepted him as imperfect. Even if they had expected him to be a model Christian and he'd failed, it wasn't likely they would have kicked his dad out of the pulpit. They sure hadn't when he was making headlines.

He'd let the car go quiet. When he parked in the Rowes' driveway, he glanced back at Ruthy and she looked as though she might start crying.

Her downturned lips propelled him out of the car and around to her door. He wrenched open the handle, unbuckled her seat belt and scooped her up for a tight hug. "I love you so much."

Her arms wrapped snugly around his neck. She shoved her forehead against his jaw. "She smells like cinnamon, Daddy."

"I know, baby. I know." He patted her back and then set her on the ground.

Mrs. Rowe trotted out before he could make it to the walkway leading to their house. "My lovely girls! I have so much planned for us today. Thank you so much for agreeing to come over, Mrs. Ashby."

"Call me Susan."

After going back to the car for the box of toys, he left and headed to the other end of town. To the inn. To home.

But doubt started to bite at his ankles like an attack dog. He'd chalked up Ruthy's shyness to that being her personality, but what if she'd needed more attention? More care? She seemed to be more affected by not having a mom. Much more so than bubbly Skylar. Although perhaps Skylar hid her pain in other ways—overtalking could be her way of dealing. They were kids, so it wasn't as though they were consciously choosing to react in those ways, but the human mind proved amazing at protecting itself from hurt.

Maggie's influence and acceptance had helped both of the girls. Skylar was more responsible and respectful now, and Ruthy no longer had to be attached to Kellen in order to talk to someone.

He left his car near the cottage and went inside to grab his journal and two permanent markers before heading over to the inn. Stopping on the porch, he braced a hand on one of the support posts and bowed his head. *You do all things for a reason. Please let Maggie be a part of the reason why my family ended up here.*

"Too afraid to come in all of a sudden?" Shoulder wedged against the doorframe, Maggie grinned at him. "Sorry I took off on you last time we were talking. I was having…a moment, for lack of a better word. I'm better now. Promise." She had a dish towel over her shoulder, her hair half pulled back in a clip and flour on her elbows. In that moment, he'd never seen someone more beautiful.

When he just stood there staring at her, she shifted her weight and pulled the dishrag off her shoulder, dusting off her hands. "What were you doing out here anyway?"

He finally found his voice. "Praying."

"Where are the girls?"

"My mom and them are at the Rowes'." He finished walking up the steps. "Maggie…would you be willing to spend the day with me?"

"Today?" She patted her hair. "Right now?" She adjusted her shirt. "I'd have to change. Get ready. I'm a mess."

He snatched her hand away from her hair, flipped it over and pressed a quick kiss to her palm. Her eyes went wide and her jaw dropped open.

"You're perfect as is." He tugged her inside. "Come with me. I thought of something that might help you with some of the changes happening in here."

Kellen led her upstairs to the area under construction. He handed her one of the hard hats that were stacked outside the area separated from the stairs by heavy plastic drapes. The plastic barrier kept the dust to a minimum. At some point, Maggie might have to temporarily move out, but they were trying to avoid that.

Hard hats on, Kellen took her hand again and lifted the plastic curtain so they could step onto the other side. "I have an idea that might sound crazy." He tugged the journal and markers from his back pocket. "But now that the place is down to studs I wanted to write Bible verses on the wood and pray in each room for all the people that will come to our inn."

"You care about the guests?"

"A lot, actually. I keep thinking about that passage in the New Testament that tells us to practice hospitality. Well, we have a really tangible opportunity to do that, right here, if we're willing to work together and compromise. Can you partner with me in this, Maggie?" He held out his hand, offering her a marker.

"Hand me that." She snatched one of the markers. "This is the best idea I've ever heard. I'll go first." She sprawled out on the floor and in huge letters wrote Zephaniah 3:17. "This is my favorite verse."

The Lord your God is with you. He is mighty to save. He will take great delight in you. He will quiet you with his love. He will rejoice over you with song.

Kellen watched her. "That's perfect."

"Wow. This really *is* helping me feel better." Maggie smiled up at him. "Your turn!"

He squatted at the entrance to the room and wrote Deuteronomy 28:6, *You will be blessed when you come in and blessed when you go out.*

They spent the next hour filling each of the guest rooms with verses and then praying in each room. When they were back in the kitchen, Maggie offered him some sun tea and asked if he wanted her to start on lunch.

"Actually—" he eased the cup out of her hand and set it in the sink "—I thought we could drive into town. There's an art fair in the square today. Let's pick out a new painting for each of the guest rooms."

"I don't know how you want to style them."

Should he tell her now about the trunk full of hundred-year-old photos he'd found in the attic after she stormed out on him? No, he couldn't ruin the surprise yet.

He shrugged. "We'll see what strikes us."

Hopefully she'd be ecstatic when she found out he'd selected pictures from the trunk to serve as inspiration for each new guest room's theme. Photos of her ancestors. But he wanted to keep that secret until he could walk her into the finished rooms.

However, there were secrets he could tell her now.

When they climbed into the car, Kellen took a deep breath. "There's something I need to come clean about. I've wanted to tell you for weeks… It's really not a big deal."

"Then just say it."

"When I inherited the inn it came with strings attached."

"Strings?"

"Namely…you."

Maggie angled her body so she could face him more. "I'm not following."

"Ida had a paragraph written into the will that said I

could inherit the inn as long as I provided a place for you and a job. It's not a big deal."

"Would you have fired me if it hadn't been for that?"

Be honest. "Probably. But, Maggie, I didn't know you. All I knew was that she'd written you into her will and I was left to wonder if you knew or not. Or if you'd used her."

"Used her?" Maggie's voice ratcheted up a notch.

The conversation wasn't going as planned. "Listen. Before I came here that's what I saw women doing. Using people to get ahead or to have money. So I just figured…"

"If anyone is using Ida it's you."

"Excuse me?"

"I took care of her. I loved her like she was my family." She clutched her purse to her chest. "You? You walked in here without a care about her and happily took hold of everything she loved without regard for it."

"Ouch." Kellen parked along the edge of the square. "For what it's worth, I'm sorry I ever acted like that."

She'd already gotten out of the car and was walking toward the fair. Kellen bolted out of the driver's seat and caught up to her. "Maggie?"

She stopped and looked at him. "For what it's worth, I forgive you for keeping that from me, but you could have saved me from a lot of anxiety if you'd told me from the get-go I wasn't about to lose my job."

He hadn't realized he'd been holding his breath. "It's worth a lot. A whole lot. But if you forgive me, why do you still look angry?"

"Forgiveness doesn't automatically change everything and make it better. It just means I won't hold it against you going forward. It doesn't mean the relationship has to stay the same." She looked away from him.

"What do you see happening with our relationship? What would you think if—"

"Can we talk about this later?" Clearly still upset, Maggie cut him a *don't speak about this in public* glare.

Had the truth just cost him and his girls the best part of Goose Harbor? No, he wouldn't let that happen. Going forward, no more secrets between them.

Chapter Fourteen

Maggie glanced over at Kellen while they stood in a booth dedicated to paintings of cats sleeping in the sunshine.

She'd been foisted onto Kellen. Like one of the unwanted stray cats in the paintings they were looking at. He'd been stuck with her. Forced to take care of her.

It was downright embarrassing.

Being pitied was far worse than being unloved.

If he'd had his way, she would have been tossed out with Ida's yellow oven and teacup collection. Did he still regret having to provide her with a job? What had Ida been thinking? Maggie didn't need to depend on a man's care to survive. She never had before. She could make do, even if that meant working the late shift at one of the diners in town again and taking Caleb and Paige up on their offer to let her stay at their house.

The cat pictures were making her sad, so she spun in the opposite direction and stalked off to a booth across the way. Kellen trailed her. The paintings looked oddly familiar. Something about the mixture of techniques and colors reminded her of…

"Alan." She almost choked on his name as the man

who'd left her so many years ago appeared from the back of the tent.

"Maggie." A smile parted Alan's signature red beard. "I was hoping I'd run into you."

"Were you?" She swallowed hard. Not because she was nervous or still cared about him. That was long past. No, that wasn't the emotion she felt. What should someone say to the man who walked off with her money, dreams and her heart and never returned?

Kellen angled his body to stand between them. "As in *Alan* Alan?"

Maggie laid a hand on Kellen's arm to let him know she was fine. "Kellen, could you give us a few minutes?"

Kellen turned toward her, a storm passing over his eyes. His eyebrows were drawn low as he worked his jaw back and forth. "Are you sure you want me to go?"

"Yes."

He nodded and then stalked off.

Alan waited until Kellen was out of earshot. "I've wanted to apologize to you for a long time. I feel... Listen, what I did to you was horrible."

Maggie forced a smile even though ten different emotions fought like overtired children in her heart. "It was a long time ago. Looks like you've done well for yourself."

"I have my own gallery in New York."

The gallery development must have been recent. She hadn't located that information the last time she'd searched for him a few years back. "That's impressive, but I'm not surprised. I always said you had the talent."

"You believed in me when no one else did."

And then he left. "I'm glad things worked out how they did." Except for the whole running-off-with-her-money part, but the middle of an art fair wasn't the best time to have that type of discussion. She'd find out where he was staying and try to catch him when there were fewer people around. "I was never meant to leave Goose Harbor and you were never meant to stay."

"Come on, Maggie, let's talk straight. The West Mansion—that pile of wood—was more important to you than anything. I could never have gotten you to leave it."

"Is that what you really think?" She'd been mourning her mother and grandmother when he left. How could he say something like that? "I stayed for people."

He grimaced. "People? Wasn't I a person? Didn't my dreams matter?"

"Of course you were—are." She was having a hard time concentrating as she scanned the crowd for Kellen. She'd stood in the way of Kellen's dreams since he set foot in Goose Harbor. She'd threatened to leave over him remodeling the mansion. His dream mattered, too. She needed to make sure Kellen understood that.

"But I wasn't worth leaving for." Alan opened up a folder and pulled out an envelope. "This is the reason I signed up for this fair. Why I traveled back." He handed it to her. "I've regretted how I ended things with you for a long time and what I did to you. I'm sorry. You have no idea how sorry, and I just wanted you to hear that."

"I forgave you a long time ago." Maggie glanced at the envelope. "What's in here?"

"What I owe you. I should have come back years ago and given you that. And just so you know, I won't take it back. Not a cent. My gallery is very lucrative." He pointed at her and smiled. "Take care of yourself. I promise not to pop back into town again without warning."

Maggie snuck away to the gazebo on the edge of the square and ripped open the envelope in private. A check for sixty thousand dollars trembled in her hands. Twenty grand more than she'd originally lent him.

She looked up and her gaze collided with Kellen's. He strode toward her but was still a good twenty yards or more away. Maggie folded up the check and slipped it into her purse.

With the money, she could be independent if she wanted to be. She could free Kellen from Ida's will. She'd have to make sure he knew that she'd decided to back him on the remodeling, and yet she knew she had to leave the West Oaks Inn. The place belonged to Kellen. His girls should be living there. It was their heritage now—not hers.

Only by leaving could she discover if Kellen really cared about her or simply felt duty-bound.

"Are you going to tell me what he said?" Kellen sucked in deep breaths through his nose as he drove.

"He came to apologize for the way he left and for disappearing."

"Good, but he's more than ten years late. Did you tell him that?"

Cool down.

But he couldn't. His heart pounded like a snare drum—deep and loud. Every time a girl had to choose between two men, Kellen lost. It had happened twice in high school and then with Cynthia. If Alan asked, would Maggie take him back?

"He hurt me in the past, but the years have helped me realize it was all for the best. I can finally let go of wondering if I made the right choice by letting him go. I did."

"So he's off the hook? Just like that? What about all the money he took from you?"

"He paid me back. With interest."

"W-with interest?" Kellen's palms were sweating on the wheel. If she had money, she could leave. Just as Cynthia had. Just as everyone always did.

"It's my turn to ask your forgiveness."

"What for?"

"I've been standing in the way of everything you've tried to do with the inn. Of your dreams. I won't be doing that anymore."

What was she saying? It felt as if she were tying up strings on the end of a package.

He'd give anything to have her fighting him again. Fighting was better than leaving. So much better. At least fighting meant she cared. "I don't mind." *Just stay.* "Stand in the way all you want. It keeps life interesting."

"I think we need some distance. With the money Alan gave me I can strike out on my own and rent a place in town. It'll buy me some time in case I don't find a new job right away. You know, I've never traveled. Maybe I will."

Money. There it was.

Kellen's knuckles turned white on the steering wheel. She'd been handed money and now she didn't need him. "So that's just it? You don't need me anymore? I get it. Another guy gave you a wad of cash and now you can leave."

"*A wad of cash?* You make it sound dirty. Like it's horrible of me to accept my own money back."

"Maybe because it is." He could have taken care of her, if Maggie had let him.

A small voice in the back of his mind reminded him that he was talking to Maggie, not Cynthia—but a wolf of fear panting down his neck told him they were one and the same. Women. All women leveled up at the first chance they could. Now Maggie could find someone without his past indiscretions. Someone without kids.

"That's not fair. You know you're not being fair." Maggie leaned against the window, away from him. "What would you have me do? Give back the money?"

"No. Take it. Have fun." Kellen unbuckled his seat belt

and got out of the car. He stalked a few feet away. *Get under control.* This was fear talking. That was what his counselor used to say. *Don't give fear a voice—only hope, speak through a megaphone of hope.* Wow. He'd messed up, hadn't he?

Maggie stood at a distance. "I can't believe you're reacting this way. You're being completely unreasonable."

"Maggie, I shouldn't have—"

She held up a hand. "Listen, we had a nice morning. Let's leave it at that. I'll still watch the girls tomorrow so you can take your mom to the airport. But let's consider this day done." She took off across the yard.

Kellen raked his hands through his hair. "Maggie! Maggie, please," he called after her, but the side door to the inn slammed.

What was wrong with him?

Chapter Fifteen

Early in the morning the clearest sounds were birds waking up and the river in the backyard slapping against the small pond mill. Today they were joined by Kellen's Subaru idling as he waited to bring his mom to the airport.

Maggie swallowed against the knot in her throat. "Safe travels. Send a note when you're home, okay?"

Susan Ashby pulled Maggie in for a tight hug. "My son is a hard nut to crack. He wouldn't admit it, but he's wounded by his past and he's scared to open up again and get rejected."

Maggie jerked her head back, talking low even though Kellen was in the car with his windows up. "Maybe if he watched his mouth a little more, he wouldn't have that problem. I'm sorry. That was rude. He and I had words yesterday."

Susan nodded. "I know. Be patient with him, but firm." His mom held on to her arms. "He needs you to let him love you."

"Love?" Maggie stepped back, breaking contact. Susan was a sweet lady, but a bit confused. Kellen love her? Not likely. They'd known each other for only a little more than two months. And not on a romantic level. No, that ship had passed by Maggie a long time ago. All ports were closed. No, it was time for Maggie to move on. Yesterday had confirmed that for her. As much as she loved the inn, she couldn't live there anymore, and if Kellen was going to continue acting out the pain of his past relationships on her, then she couldn't work there any longer, either. She'd decide about the job later, but for now she was almost certain she'd leave the private portion of the inn.

Susan picked up her hand gently and cradled it in her own. "Ida and I have been praying for the two of you for years. She might have given the inn to Kellen to provide for his girls, but she did it just as much to take care of you. Through him."

Praying for the two of them for years? Maggie's mind spun. She wanted to ask what Susan meant, but all she could muster was "He's...he's a great boss."

"Oh, he's more than that." Susan waggled her eyebrows. "I do believe with his newfound faith, he's going to make you an excellent husband. Just as Ida always said. He'll need loads of patience, of course."

Love? Husband?

Maggie shook her head. "I think you're confused. This is Kellen we're talking about. Ex-rocker Kellen Ashby, who was a lead singer. I've read the articles. He was fawned over by women. He's dated movie stars."

Susan looked up and to the left. "Well, yes, there was that one. But she was a C-lister at best, and it was one date. The papers try to make things in Hollywood into bigger deals than they are. They met in a grocery store. He asked her out. All she talked about was how attractive the hero of the latest movie was. They never talked again."

"Which is fine. But I can't compare with the girls I've seen pictures of."

"You're right." Susan nodded. "You can't."

Ouch. Maggie's heart plummeted to the soles of her shoes.

Susan patted her hand. "You're so far out of their league, it would be unfair to them if we tried to compare. Besides, each couple works together differently. Just because the media decides someone is a big deal, it doesn't mean they're better or worse than anyone else. And it doesn't mean they'll make a good wife or mother."

"Do you believe there's one right person for everyone?"

"I don't. And I've been happily married for forty-eight years, mind you."

"So." Maggie licked her lips. "Your husband isn't your soul mate?"

Maggie always struggled with the thought that certain people were made for each other, but her mom had told her time and again that she should wait for that *one special man.* If there was only one perfect person for everyone, then was Sarah—Caleb's first wife—his one special person, or was Paige, his second wife? Was Caleb not supposed to have married Sarah to begin with? In doing so, had he taken someone else's soul mate? Then again, without experiencing the loss of Sarah, he wouldn't have become the man who fell in love with Paige.

It was all so confusing.

Susan's smile was so kind. "I look at it like your cabinet full of pots and lids. All jumbled up together. Almost any pot and lid combination will boil water. Sure, there are some lids that'll be way too small that they'd fall in the pot, so we don't reach for those ones. But by and large, most pots and lids will work enough to get the job done."

"That kind of kills my dream of romance."

"Oh, not at all. Choosing to love someone—bruises and all—is the most romantic thing in the world. It makes a marriage the most beautiful part of life." Susan looped her arm through Maggie's and walked her closer to the car. "I'm just saying, once you pick who you're going to love and commit yourself to, a marriage can work. There is no perfect lid. Too many young people are waiting for *perfect*, and that doesn't exist. That's all I'm saying. We're all sinners, and sinners make mistakes and fail each other. Marriage is about offering grace daily and loving through the hardest moments. And when it's done like that…" Susan whistled. "Romance is everywhere."

Kellen rolled down his window. "Ma, we have to go if you're going to make your flight."

Susan pulled Maggie in for one last hug. "See you at Thanksgiving if not before then. Oh, what am I saying? We'll see you before then. I have a feeling fall will be a good time for a wedding."

Just humor her until she's gone.

Maggie waved, watching them pull away before heading over to the cottage. She opened the door as quietly as she could. The kittens, Pete and Repeat, greeted her, curling around her legs mewing as she entered.

It was far too early in the morning to wake the girls. They'd said their goodbyes to their grandmother over a pecan pie at the inn last night.

"Shhh, boys. I'll get you some food in a second, but let's not wake Skylar and Ruthy, okay?" She scooped up the two balls of fluff. They erupted in purrs.

She couldn't recognize the cottage as Ida's anymore. This was the Ashbys' home now. Pink and yellow paint had been replaced by warm earth tones. A huge painting of a desert filled the back wall. Kellen had grown up in Arizona. Did he miss it? She traced her fingers over the back of the soft leather couch. Three different guitars rested on stands in the back corner next to a small area he'd turned into an office. There was an Apple computer with a microphone and a piano-like keyboard attached to it. Toys spilled from a huge plastic toy box near the television.

The place was far too small for his family's needs. It had been a picture-perfect home for Ida and Henry, but not for Kellen, his girls and the kittens. Maggie should have offered them the private part of the inn when they'd first moved. As much as she loved the connection to her family, it had been selfish to remain there when Kellen, Skylar and Ruthy needed it. Seeing how squashed they were confirmed it. She'd start looking for a place to rent next week and make arrangements in the next month to be out of the inn.

Entering the kitchen, she was determined to busy herself until either Kellen returned or the girls woke up, but she found the sink empty and everything in order. A small table with two chairs gathered around it fit snugly by the back window. Kellen's huge coffee mug sat there, with a half cup of his favorite brew growing cold. Maggie crossed to the table and snapped a lid over his travel mug. He'd probably meant to bring it along and forgot to. She was about to put it in the fridge, but she spotted his Bible and what looked like a journal resting on the chair.

She made eye contact with Repeat, the little orange kitten. "I shouldn't snoop. I really shouldn't."

But a Bible wasn't private, was it?

The pages were dog-eared and the Bible was twice as big as it should have been because every other page had a Post-it stuck to it or a piece of paper with notes scribbled on it shoved inside. Maggie smiled. So Kellen wasn't *always* organized. A single sheet of computer paper lay under his journal. She moved the journal to the side. She wouldn't look in there. No doubt that was private.

SG with a question mark was written at the top of the page along with a few incomplete sentences. Scanning the list, she leaned against the wall and slowly dropped to the floor.

Leave Maggie.

Sell the inn.

Girls with Mom and Dad?

The muscles in her shoulders went hard and she worked her jaw back and forth, wanting to yell but not doing so because of two sleeping girls. Daughters it looked as though he was planning to shove off on his parents at some point. Why?

It didn't matter. She'd been right all along.

An artist through and through, just like Alan. Goose Harbor would never be good enough for Kellen to call home. He was passing through. Using it as a stepping-stone to something else. Kellen's plan wasn't to continue being an inn owner. He'd lied to her when he said he cared about their future guests. He was going to rebrand it and sell it for top dollar. Leaving Maggie high and dry with nothing just as Alan had done. Not that Kellen owed her anything. But he should have warned her. Should have told her to start looking for another living situation. Another job.

Why would he hire Nika just to sell the place? Unless she was part of the rebranding. Maybe he'd assure her a position with whoever bought the place.

Maybe Maggie could make an offer to purchase it from him? She could probably secure a loan using the money Alan had paid back as a down payment. Who was she kidding? She didn't know the first thing about running a business.

Forget making arrangements in the next month. She needed to leave. Now.

Shoving the page under his journal, she yanked her phone out of her back pocket and pulled up Paige's number. Her friend wouldn't be awake yet, but Maggie wanted her to get the message right away.

When can I move in?

The girls still hadn't woken up when Kellen returned. Which was a good thing because after finding Kellen's cruel list, she wasn't in the best mood for entertaining kids.

Maggie waited only until he'd parked the car before smoothing down her hair and opening the door. Kellen was still in the driveway, his phone to his ear.

"I can have it cleared out by the end of the month." He paused.

Maggie froze.

"I'm perfectly happy with that price. Honestly I'll be glad to have the place off my hands."

Sell the inn.

So he'd already worked out a deal to sell the inn? When was he going to tell her? As far as he knew, she'd still planned on continuing on at the inn. Well, no longer. Good thing she'd found the note in his house. If not, she wouldn't have been able to bite her tongue after listening to his phone conversation.

She prowled back across the yard, making sure to let the gate between their yards creak loud enough for him to hear it so he wouldn't think she'd abandoned Skylar and Ruthy before he'd returned. No, abandoning was Kellen's style. Not hers.

Girls with Mom and Dad?

Back in the inn's kitchen, she eased the door shut and then ran to her room. Without stopping to think, she yanked her suitcase out of her closet, opened up a drawer and shoved everything inside. She needed to leave before she saw him again.

How dare Kellen take away her right to leave her old home on her own terms! He was selfish and cruel—just what she'd originally pegged him as.

Tears dropped in along with her belongings, but she didn't care. She needed to get things packed and get on the road to Paige and Caleb's as quickly as possible.

She rubbed the ache in her chest. Why did it hurt so much?

Despite trying to guard her heart, she'd gone and developed feelings for Kellen. Even now, losing the inn didn't bother her as much as realizing that he'd never meant to stay. That he'd used her to pass time. Well, *used* was a harsh term for his actions. Kellen hadn't been overly romantic.

Yet he'd stolen her heart.

Maggie dropped down on the bed.

Each time he'd taken her hand to pray with her or share what God had been teaching him. Whenever he sent her a smile across the dinner table. The few hugs and time holding hands. That had been enough for Maggie to feel involved with him—to grow attached. More than attached... to fall in love.

Groaning, she buried her head in her hands.

Why did it always have to be the unstable artist?

Kellen Ashby didn't want her. Six years older than him, with crow's-feet showing around her eyes—how had she ever allowed herself to hope? To believe he could care for her?

"Such foolishness." She shoved the butts of her hands into her eyes. "He could never love me."

Kellen had lied and led her on. They'd prayed and written verses upstairs, and that whole time he knew he had a deal in the works. Once again, she'd put her hope in the wrong sort of man. Not again.

Never again.

"Maggie?" Kellen's voice. Why hadn't she locked the doors?

"Busy," she growled and went back to packing.

"Please. Can we talk?"

She braced her hands on the edge of her suitcase. *Don't look at him.* "Leave."

"Maggie—"

"Don't you get it? I don't want to talk to you." She spun around and stalked toward her closet. Hopefully he wouldn't come into her bedroom.

"What are you doing?" His voice held a raw, nervous edge.

Don't grow soft. He'd destroyed Ida's belongings along with Maggie's ancestral home. He'd kept the terms of the will from her even though they'd involved her—allowing her to unnecessarily worry about losing her job for weeks. And he'd already plotted out his escape plan to unload the inn and leave Goose Harbor. Everything pointed to the fact that he'd never cared about Maggie. Not at all.

"Packing. Clearly." She shoved some shoes into her bag as her phone started to ring. Paige's name showed up on the screen. "Paige? Thank you for calling me."

"I got your message about moving in. Caleb and I are happy to have you, but it came as a surprise. The last time I talked to you, everything sounded fine."

That was before Kellen had proven to be a liar. "Things changed."

"Okay. Well, when we get back we'll get the room ready for you. It's a wreck at the moment. Does next weekend work?"

Weekend? A quiet panic swirled around her heart. "I was hoping today."

"Oh. Caleb and I are out of town. The principal sent

us to a school safety conference and we'll be here for the next three days. I didn't leave a spare key with anyone or else I'd have them let you in. I'm sorry. We should have thought to give you one."

Maggie pressed her hand over her forehead. "The weekend will be fine." She could rent a room at a hotel. No, she couldn't. The town would never stop talking about her if word got out that she'd left the West Oaks Inn and stayed somewhere else. She'd leave quietly, with as few public ripples in the water as she could.

"All right, we'll touch base when we get back on Thursday, okay?"

"Talk to you then."

Maybe Kellen had left. Maggie glanced over her shoulder, and her heart lodged into her throat. No—he was there. Still in her doorway with his hands shoved into his pockets. Looking way too handsome.

Maggie went back to her suitcase and closed the lid. "You need to go back to the cottage. The girls are alone."

He rocked on his feet. "Will you come with me so we can talk?"

"Frankly I'd be fine never talking to you again."

His face fell. "Maggie…what's going on?"

Finally facing him, she popped her hands onto her hips. "Sell me the inn."

"What?" He scrunched his brow. "No. I can't."

"Of course you can't." Because he'd already sold it. "I knew it."

"I'm so confused right now, but the one thing I know is that I don't want to lose you."

"Well, seeing as you can't lose something you never had, I think you'll be just fine." Unshed tears swam in her vision. "Now I need you to leave. I need you to leave and not come back until next weekend. Can you do that for me?"

He moved to come into her room and stopped himself. "You're freaking me out. What are you talking about?"

"I know the inn is yours and all, but can you just promise me you won't come into my home—my only sanctuary on earth—until I've moved out? It's not like you're needed in the private part of the inn right now. Use the front door and check on the inn's construction all you want." *Please. Please just agree to this.* She wouldn't be able to handle seeing him every day.

"Listen, I'm sorry I snapped at you about the money from Alan. I couldn't care less about it. It just brought back memories of when Cynthia left me. I was afraid that if you didn't depend on me, then you wouldn't stay."

Say something that'll make him go. Shut down the conversation.

"Looks like you were right." *Leave him before he can do it first.* He *was* planning to leave after all. She wouldn't be played the lovesick girl again.

Kellen's head jerked back. "Oh. You don't…? I thought…" He backed into the hallway.

Don't show emotion. "I don't."

"I had thought…hoped. I guess I was wrong." He pinched the bridge of his nose. "I'm sorry to have taken up your time. I won't come here until Saturday."

As he walked away, Maggie sank onto her bed and fisted the comforter into her hands, anchoring herself to keep from following after him. From yelling out that she wasn't being truthful. That she loved him and was terrified for him to leave Goose Harbor and never return.

Leave Maggie.

At least he wouldn't be able to tick that one off his list. She'd left him first.

Chapter Sixteen

Maggie jolted awake.

It sounded like a bull ramming into her house. Pounding. That was someone at the side door. She squinted at her alarm clock. Three in the morning.

"Who could possibly—"

"Maggie! Open up."

Kellen.

She shoved off her blankets and tossed on a thin long-sleeved shirt. Fumbling, she ran into the kitchen. For Kellen to be at her door at such a time in the night, something had to be dreadfully wrong. Especially after their fight two days ago. True to his word, they hadn't seen each other since he left the inn.

A peek through the curtains showed Kellen—eyes wide and hair rumpled—holding Skylar in his arms.

Maggie flung open the door. "What's wrong?"

"I know I said I wouldn't come until Saturday, but something happened. Can you stay with Ruthy?" He was breathing hard.

"Yes, but—"

"My arm huuurrts." Skylar cried against her dad's shoulder.

Kellen turned and strode back into the darkness between their yards. "Come on."

Barefoot, Maggie jogged to catch up to him. She fought against a shiver. It might have been spring, but the nights were still chilly. "What happened?"

"Sky fell out of her bunk bed and hit her arm. I think… it looks broken."

"Should I call for an ambulance?" She hadn't thought to bring her phone.

Kellen nodded in a chin-up way to indicate his car. "I'm bringing her to the hospital. As long as you'll stay with Ruthy. She's still asleep. She slept through everything."

"Of course. For as long as you need." She held open the car's back door.

Kellen buckled Skylar into her booster seat.

Skylar moaned and cradled her arm to her chest. "It hurts, Daddy."

"I know, baby." He dropped a kiss on her temple. "Let's get you to a doctor."

Maggie had one arm resting on the top of the car and the other holding the door, so when Kellen stood and turned around, he was basically in her arms. Maggie removed her arms quickly.

"Sorry." Kellen brushed past. "I know you don't like contact with me."

They were gone before Maggie made it to the front door of the cottage. The house detailed the Ashbys' evening. Cold mugs with leftover hot-chocolate rings in the bottom sat on the coffee table, and a bowl of half-eaten popcorn sat near a DVD case. A few Disney character–themed blankets and stuffed animals littered the floor, and the kittens were curled up together on a side chair. Looked as though the girls had enjoyed a movie date with their dad. Kellen really was a good father.

As it was still nighttime, her best course of action was probably to curl up on the couch and fall back to sleep. Not yet. Maggie propped her hands on her hips and studied the room again. If only she could find out where he was planning to go once he left Goose Harbor. Was he rejoining the Snaggletooth Lions? It would need to be something like that for him to need Skylar and Ruthy to live with his parents.

She gathered the bowl and mugs and brought them into the kitchen. After unloading their dishwasher, sweeping the floor and wiping down the counters in the kitchen, she moved into the living room and started picking up all the toys. There was still the bathroom, but Maggie didn't want to risk waking up Ruthy by turning on the water. Her bedroom shared a wall with the bathroom.

Feeling restless and not at all like sleeping, Maggie trailed her fingers over the jewel cases stacked two deep in the small bookshelf near Kellen's computer. A larger bookshelf spanned the length of the wall, but that one, like the one in Maggie's home, held books. While Maggie liked a good book now and then, she was more interested in Kellen's music collection. What made him tick? He clearly loved music. Reading the lyrics to the Snaggletooth Lions' first album had shown her how talented he was. And his voice. The man could sing instead of talk every day going forward and the world would be better for it. His speaking voice held a melodic quality, too. Seriously, the man could read books on tape for a living.

On top of his keyboard rested a CD. Maggie picked it up. It had no words written on it, but the area near the middle was darker, so it had been recorded on. What type of music did he listen to now? Did he miss his old rocker days?

Before she had time to consider what she was doing, Maggie shoved the CD into the computer and pressed Play.

Over the speakers, a guitar started playing a song she wasn't familiar with. It was beautiful and relaxing. She rolled her shoulders, leaned back in the computer chair and closed her eyes.

When I thought You left me, I'm the one who walked away. Me who didn't trust.

Yet You're here. Always here.

Waiting. Watching. Loving. Knowing.

I will come back to You, my first love. My only. I'll come back to You.

Kellen's rich voice washed over her as she repeated the words in her heart. How many times would it take her to realize she had to trust God completely? Sure, she'd tossed the words out before. But deep down, had she believed them? The world and every part of it that she loved felt as if it were being torn away. Beyond that, if she was being honest, she felt let down by God. She'd followed what she thought was right in the Bible and instead of being blessed she'd lost her family, been passed in love twice and was about to lose her home forever.

And Kellen and the girls. For the past month or two they'd felt like a family. A real, imperfect but loving family. But now she'd lost that, too. She'd thought she'd made some spiritual progress, but perhaps she hadn't after all. What was the point in having hope anymore?

Those thoughts wouldn't help her. No, dwelling on that pattern would sink her soul further into discouragement. Mom had always told her to take every thought captive and examine it to see if she was allowing herself to believe a lie or not.

How had Maggie forgotten about that?

I will come back to You, my first love. My only. I'll come back to You.

She needed to start choosing to see the ways God was

working. Really look and notice the opportunities and the ways He was guiding her even when it didn't feel as if He cared or was there. Face it—she had no control over her circumstances, so dwelling on them wasn't beneficial. But she could control her attitude and perspective.

God was doing something new. She could embrace it or fight it. The choice was hers.

Praise-and-worship song after song tumbled from the computer speakers. Maggie prayed through each of them. Kellen had a gift. An amazing gift. And he needed to use it. Maybe he was using it. Perhaps he'd written these songs to sell or with a band in mind. Perhaps that was why he was leaving. And if that was the case…could she blame him? The man had raw and wonderful talent.

The final song on the CD wasn't exactly a praise-and-worship song. It was a love song. Maggie strained to hear all the words. Kellen sang about two imperfect people chasing hand in hand after God. The words talked about a forever kind of love that forgave daily.

It was the kind of love Maggie had been searching for her entire life.

"Maggie?" A small, sleepy voice broke her concentration.

Maggie swiveled in her chair. Standing in the entrance to the room from the hallway, Ruthy rubbed her eyes, a big stuffed bunny snug under one arm.

"Sweetheart, let's get you back into bed."

"Where's my daddy?"

Don't let Ruthy worry.

Maggie kept her voice soft and even. "Skylar got hurt and he needed to take her to the doctor."

Ruthy shuffled into the room. "Is she going to be okay?"

"I think so. She was very brave." Maggie stood, stretching. A couple pops sounded from her back. "Let's get you settled back in bed."

"Doesn't Daddy's voice make you happy?" Ruthy grinned as the song went through its last chorus.

"It does."

"Can we listen to it again?" Ruthy pointed to the computer. The CD had ended.

Maggie leaned back and clicked for the playlist to start over. "Sure thing. Here, let's get more comfortable so we can get sleepy again and go back to bed." Maggie held out her hand and led Ruthy over to the couch. "Why don't you lie down and I'll put a blanket on you?"

"Will you sit with me?"

Trying to make the atmosphere conducive to getting a child back to sleep, Maggie dimmed a light and turned off the rest. When she sat down on the couch, Ruthy immediately crawled onto her lap and rested her head against her shoulder. Maggie must have picked the seat that Kellen normally sat in, because the fabric on the couch smelled like his cologne. She pulled a pillow under her arm and took a deep breath. Lemon and after rain. The best smell in the world.

She shoved the pillow away. Being in his home while trying to get over her feelings for him wasn't helping.

"Do you want to listen to Daddy sing forever?" Ruthy whispered.

Maggie blinked against the burn rising in her eyes. "I do, sweetheart. I really do."

And she did. She wanted to be teased by him for taking on too many things at once; she wanted him to reorganize her spice cabinet for the third time; she wanted to hear more of his insights on the Bible and be the first one to hear his new songs for the rest of her life. More than that, though, she wanted to tuck Ruthy and Skylar in each night and make them breakfast each morning. To hug them tight when they left for school and be someone they could share their stories with when they got home. Family. All of it.

Her dreams were right here in the cottage and she couldn't have them. And that was what hurt the most.

Ruthy's deep, even breaths told Maggie she'd fallen asleep. Maggie leaned her head down, smelling Ruthy's hair. The girls must use bubble-gum-scented shampoo.

She wanted to be knit together into their lives.

But that would never be possible, would it? One more hope that would never happen. One more disappointment. One more opportunity to see her dream and have it ripped away.

Don't think that way! She'd just decided to change her perspective and attitude, hadn't she? But she saw words written in her mind: *Leave Maggie. Sell the inn. Girls with Mom and Dad?*

Clearly Kellen was going somewhere. They'd had their moments, both good and bad, but Kellen didn't want Maggie.

No one did. Well, no one but God. He cared.

She wouldn't doubt that again.

Kellen pushed the rounded door open with his foot as he cradled Skylar. She'd sleep late tomorrow—or was it already today? He'd call her in sick to school and she could relax at home with him and Ruthy.

No doubt she'd want to run over to Maggie's and show off her pink camo cast once she was up. Maggie would be great about it. She'd ooh and aah over the plaster and draw a picture on the cast. She was always so kind with his girls; her affection for them was clear. Kellen wished she felt the same way about him, but she'd made it pretty clear that she'd never harbored any romantic leanings toward him.

His eyes were adjusted to the dark from the long drive.

He maneuvered around furniture, went straight to his bedroom and put his sleeping daughter in his bed. He'd crash on the couch tonight because he wasn't about to chance Skylar falling out of the bunk bed again. In the morning he'd check the guardrail and see what had come loose to allow the accident to happen. In the meantime, she was safe in his room.

Kellen rubbed his face and went back to the living room. The sight that met him made him stop in his tracks. Maggie, head tipped back and mouth slightly open, slept on the couch with Ruthy and their black kitten, Pete, cradled against her. Even in the dim light, Maggie's cheeks were flushed from the warmth of holding Ruthy. Kellen's heart twisted. He loved her. There, he'd finally acknowledged it. Not that acknowledging it changed that she didn't want him.

As he gently scooped Ruthy into his arms, Maggie stirred. He'd missed being near to her the past few days. What would he do when she left?

When he returned, Maggie was still on the couch, rubbing her eyes. Looking even more adorable than his daughters looked when they were tired. Kellen fought the urge to go to her.

Bracing her hands on the coffee table, Maggie stood. "How's Skylar?"

"Just a hairline fracture. She's pretty psyched about the cast, though."

"I'm glad she's okay. Well, good night. Get some sleep." Maggie rounded the back side of the couch, away from him, and headed to the door.

He slipped outside behind her. "I know it's late and we're both tired, but can we talk?"

Shivering a little, she crossed her arms. "What about?"

Kellen slipped out of his fleece jacket and draped it

over her shoulders. She might have long sleeves on, but the fabric was thin and her bare feet weren't helping her stay warm in dawn's bite of cold air.

"Your feet. Do you want some shoes?"

She glanced down as if just noticing for the first time that she hadn't worn shoes. "I'll live." She shuffled so her feet were off the stone porch and resting on the welcome mat. "What's up?"

Wanting to be able to see her face, Kellen closed the distance between them. He ran his hands down her arms and took hold of both her hands. She might not care about him, but if this could be his last chance to hold her, he'd take it. "Why do you want to leave the inn?"

Maggie bit her lip. "You're making this so hard."

"What's hard about it?" He squeezed her hand. "You can tell me anything."

She jerked her hands away. "You can't do this, Kellen. Don't you see? You can't take my hand and speak softly and make me hope for things. I know you're leaving. I know you planned that all along. And if you're telling me you sold the inn, well, I already heard that so—"

He stepped closer. "I'm not selling the inn."

"I heard you on the phone selling it!"

He raised his eyebrows. "I promise, I'm not."

"But I *heard* you talking to someone on the phone about agreeing to a price and you said you'd move out for them."

The pieces were starting to click together. No wonder she'd been so upset on Sunday. "That conversation you heard… I'm going to rent the cottage to the man the church committee just announced is going to be taking the position as pastor at the new church. He's young and newly married. It'll be a good space for them."

"You're not selling the inn?" Suddenly her bare feet became the most important things in the world.

"I'm not." He tentatively picked up her hand again. "Is that why you were angry at me?"

"Not just that." She took a deep breath. "When I was at your house the other day I snooped a bit and found your Bible and journal." She plunged ahead before he could speak. "I didn't read your journal, but there was a list on a piece of paper and you had things like *sell the inn* and *leave Maggie* on there."

He should probably be bothered that she'd pawed through his personal stuff, but he wasn't. They didn't need secrets between them. If he really wanted to pursue a relationship with her, he'd not make the same mistakes that had plagued his time with Cynthia.

"So you only saw my cons list and decided that I'd made up my mind?" He moved his hand under her chin and leaned even closer so they shared the same air. "Had you opened up my journal and read where I write out my prayers, you would have found in the latest one that day that I hadn't needed to finish the sheet because I'd already made up my mind and a pro-and-con list wouldn't have changed that."

She licked her lips. "What did you decide?"

He dropped his hand so he could slip it under the fleece coat to rest on the small of her back. "That no matter how tempting an opportunity might be, my place is here. Indefinitely."

"Was it the Snaggletooth Lions? Did they want you back?"

Kellen pulled a face. "Snaggletooth? No. I'd never. And we don't talk. Have you heard of a band called Since Grace?"

"Only the most popular touring Christian band in the world. Yeah, I might have heard of them."

"A while ago I auditioned to join them."

"Kellen!" She fisted her hands into his shirt. "Your praise-and-worship songs are so powerful."

How did she know about those? "My…"

"Tonight I listened to the CD by your computer. Hearing your music made me feel like you'd taken me by the hand and walked me right into the throne room of God. I haven't experienced anything like that before. I hope you don't mind that I listened."

"No one's ever heard that stuff." His eyes wandered to the outdoor light hanging above them. "Well, besides Sky and Ruthy."

She shook him gently where she held his shirt, making him look back at her again. "Forgive me, Kellen? I've been acting really selfish lately. God gave you an amazing gift and you need to share it with the world. I wouldn't have said this before listening to your playlist, but I understand if you want to join Since Grace. You could have such an impact on the world, and the girls will probably love staying with your parents when you tour."

"Maggie." He cocked his head. *Silly woman.* "Have you been listening to a word I've said? I turned them down. I'm staying here, in Goose Harbor. This is our home now. I won't be moving the girls anywhere else."

"But your music. You're clearly passionate about writing and performing songs."

Kellen shrugged. "I'll figure out a way to make use of that at some point. For now I'm happy to sing for my girls… for you. I'm sorry for everything I said about the money… about Alan."

"Forgiven. I understand now why you reacted that way."

"Maggie, I…I don't know how to say this." He searched her eyes as his heart blasted against his rib cage. Would she reject him?

"What?"

"I'm in love with you." He let go of her. "I mean, if you don't feel the same way I understand. I won't mention it again. It's just…we felt like a family up until the past weekend and I didn't want you to think that I only cared about you because you watch the girls. I care about *you*. I'm attracted to you. You challenge me to be a better man and to see things in a new way. You wanted to know me as an individual and it didn't impress you at all that I'd once toured. Which is a good thing. I want to be with you, but I understand—"

Maggie fisted her hands in his shirt again and jerked him forward. Her lips crashed into his before his brain could catch up. When it did, he wound his arms around her, his fingers twisting into her curls. Maggie's kiss was hungry. Searching. Kellen answered it with equal energy.

She broke away, breathing hard. "Does that answer your question?"

He rested his forehead against hers. "I don't even remember asking one."

"I'm sorry I jumped to conclusions. I should have come to you."

They both had to work on being more open. "Let's focus on right now instead of worrying about the past."

"Now what?" Maggie raised her eyebrows.

Kellen fought a growl. She had no idea how appealing she looked.

"Let's get you back home."

Maggie started to shrug out of his jacket.

He stopped her hands. "Keep it. Here, jump on my back."

"Your…back?" She dropped his hand.

"Piggyback. The ground is covered in dew and you're barefoot."

She raised one skeptical eyebrow. "You do know I'm an adult, right? And I weigh what an adult weighs."

"You're never too old for a piggyback ride."

She finally climbed onto his back and he carried her

across the yard. Maggie's laugh filled the air. With her arms wrapped around the front of his shoulders and feeling her heart beat against his back, he wouldn't have minded walking all the way to downtown Goose Harbor like that.

They were at her porch all too soon. Kellen swung her down on the last step. Relishing the moment and nearness, he stepped up to her level and wrapped his arms around her again, pulling her in for another kiss. It was short. Just a good-night. He wanted her to feel cherished...not as if he was about to maul her. He'd learned restraint since his Cynthia days.

"You are beautiful," he whispered as he stepped down off the porch.

"See you in the morning."

He hooked his fingers into his pockets. "So I don't have to obey the Saturday rule anymore?"

Maggie rolled her eyes.

"Good night." He laughed and backed away. Kellen didn't wait for her response. If he stayed any longer he'd kiss her again. And he didn't know if he'd be able to stop.

Chapter Seventeen

Maggie pulled the lace curtain away from the window of the tidy house and glanced out.

Her friend Paige patted her shoulder. "You know, a watched pot never boils."

Maggie let the curtain drop. "He said he'd be here ten minutes ago."

Paige's smile was kind, hopeful. "Kellen will be here. He's got the girls to juggle. He'd call if he had to cancel."

For the final month of the remodeling, both she and Kellen had decided that it would be best if Maggie moved out of the private side of the inn after all. Paige and Caleb had welcomed her with open arms. Her time with them had been relaxing, but she was glad it was over. Their house wasn't home. Not for Maggie.

The doorbell rang and Maggie beat Paige to the door.

She flung it open, making the elaborate flower wreath hanging on it shudder.

"Kellen," Maggie breathed. He was dressed simply in jeans and a T-shirt. He'd gotten better about following the easier dress code that reigned in Goose Harbor. Even still, he looked like a man from a magazine. The only difference was that he was holding out his hand—for her.

She placed her hand in his.

He pulled her close. "I've missed you." He pressed a quick kiss to her lips. "So much."

"This living-ten-minutes-away thing isn't cutting it, huh?" She swatted his chest.

Paige adjusted the wreath on the door and shooed them off the front steps. "You two have fun."

Kellen opened the passenger door for her, but anything he was saying was drowned out by Skylar and Ruthy greeting her as she buckled up.

Skylar squeezed her arm. "You're going to love the inn! It's all done and Daddy said we can live there now."

"I'm sure whatever your dad did was great." Maggie commanded the butterflies in her stomach to be still as she smiled back at Skylar.

While staying with Caleb and Paige, Kellen had instructed Maggie not to come to the inn. He'd said he wanted to surprise her with the transformation. The wait had been sheer torture. They'd all met for outings to the beach and dinner in town, but Maggie missed their old life as next-door neighbors. Although they'd never enjoy that again, would they? The new pastor and his wife had moved in only last week. The Ashbys were living in the inn now that the construction was complete.

Kellen claimed her hand for the drive over. "Are you nervous?"

"Not nervous." She shook her head. "Just really proud of you. Thank you for letting me share in this moment."

But nerves hit her when he parked in front of the inn. From the outside, it looked as it always had. The inside would not. She knew that and had prepared her heart that morning during her time praying and reading the Bible. Still, she wanted to be excited about the changes, for Kellen's sake, but what if she hated how it looked?

Kellen smiled at her as he led her up the front steps. "Ready?"

"Yes."

"Hold the door for us, Sky."

Skylar held open the door and Ruthy ran in ahead of them. Maggie gasped when they entered. The floors had been refinished and her great-grandfather's chandelier glistened, showing every new detail in the room. The large wall in the dining room caught her eye right away. From chair rail to close to the ceiling, old family photos were framed and beautifully hung, making the room look as though it belonged in a home-decorating magazine.

Maggie tugged on Kellen's hand, going instantly to the wall. She ran her finger over a black frame that held a picture of her grandma surrounded by chickens. "Where did you get these?"

"They were in the attic… Do you like it?"

"I love this." She blinked back tears.

Skylar hugged Maggie's leg. "If you like it, why are you crying?"

Maggie bent down and hugged Skylar tightly. "Sometimes, when our hearts are so happy, that happiness has to spill out somewhere. You make me that happy."

Skylar koala-hugged her back. "What about Daddy? Does he make you that happy?"

"He does."

"And me?" Ruthy tugged on her sleeve.

Maggie opened her arm to pull Ruthy in, as well. "You, too, sweetheart."

Ruthy nuzzled her neck and whispered, "Can I call you Mom?"

Maggie looked up at Kellen, silently asking him how she should respond. He nodded, practically beaming.

"If you want to call me Mom, I think that might just

make me happier than I've ever been in my life." Maggie pressed a kiss to each girl's head.

Kellen rested his hand on her shoulder as she rose. "Let's show you the rooms. We based the design of each guest suite off one of your family's photos."

"You didn't have to do all this. You could have followed your dream for this place."

"Maggie." He turned her gently to face him. "You're my dream now."

"I love you." It was the first time she'd said the words out loud, and Kellen looked as if he might start spilling happiness from his eyes any second.

"I love you, too."

Hearing the words made her heart jolt every time, but still, even after everything some fears lingered.

She knit her fingers together. "I'm so ordinary and you're amazing. I'm not like those other girls you dated. And I'm six years older than you. I have wrinkles here by my eyes."

He grabbed the hand that she was using to point at her wrinkles. "One—don't belittle yourself, not to me, because I won't hear it. Two—you're right. You're not like the women I've dated before…which is why I find you so attractive. Maggie, don't compare yourself to anyone, okay?" He laced his fingers with hers. "And the age thing? Yeah, I couldn't care less about that."

"It's a lot to take in. No one has been interested in me in a long, long time."

"Their loss." Kellen gave her hand an encouraging squeeze. "But you've thrown me off topic. Let's show you upstairs."

The girls pounded up the stairs and Maggie turned to join them but froze when she saw the railing. "You kept the original railing. You said you were going to destroy it. You said…" She ran her fingers over the curls in the wood.

Kellen twisted his arm around her waist, drawing her near. "It just so happens that there's a lot of stuff that came with the house that I realized I really love."

Skylar's and Ruthy's giggles trickled down the stairs. Maggie raised her eyebrows to Kellen. "Should we join them?"

"Not quite yet." His grin turned wolfish right before he stole another kiss. "I wanted to tell you before we get there—I remodeled the private side of the inn, too. I made the master suite bigger and added a bathroom. I wanted it to fit our needs better going forward."

"Our needs?" Maggie toyed with the edge of his shirt.

"I've wasted enough of my life on wrong things. I don't want to waste too much of it without you beside me. I hope that makes sense."

"Hope. That's the key going forward, isn't it?" She laced her fingers with his and pressed a kiss to the back of his hand.

"'It always protects, always trusts, always hopes, always preserves.'" He quoted from the often-dubbed "love chapter" of the Bible. 1 Corinthians 13. "Going forward, I'll love you like that."

"We're both messes at relationships, aren't we?"

"Good thing we believe in a God who happens to be an expert at fixing messes."

"It's like the song on your CD." Maggie ran her fingers down his arm. "The last song was a romantic love song about two imperfect people chasing after God."

He reached up, catching one of her curls and tucking it behind her ear. "I wrote that song for you."

"You did?" She breathed the question.

"If you had snooped in my journal, you would have known that, too."

"You're never going to let me live that down, are you?" She swatted him. "I promise, no more snooping."

He shrugged. "Ah. I don't mind." With a playful tug, he pulled her forward, making her lose her balance. Maggie landed against his chest. "We should go find the girls. They're dying to show you everything."

She splayed a hand on his heart. "Let's go see our dreams."

"Not our dreams, Maggie—our reality." He wrapped his arms around her.

Ruthy harrumphed from the top of the steps. "Come on, Mom and Dad! Come see."

Chuckling, Maggie and Kellen went upstairs and the four of them explored the new inn—as a family.

* * * * *

Dear Reader,

How do we move forward when our past has such a hold on us? The fact of the matter is, we don't. We can't. Not until we let go.

We often allow our past to color who we are now, but God says that we don't have to. Pain and mistakes made yesterday don't have to hold us back from a new life today. Isn't that amazing? The difficult part is, we have to choose to let go of the past—we have to decide that yesterday won't define who we are today.

Be brave, friends. Choose the clean slate. Don't allow a mistake from the past to hold back your dreams or your chance at love.

Thank you for spending time with Kellen and Maggie. I hope you enjoyed their story. Make sure to come back to Goose Harbor often and find out what's happening to all the other people you've met along the way. I love interacting with readers, so make sure to look me up on Facebook, Twitter or at www.jessicakellerbooks.com and say hi!

Dream Big,
Jess

COMING NEXT MONTH FROM
Love Inspired®

Available July 21, 2015

THE COWBOY'S SURPRISE BABY
Cowboy Country • by Deb Kastner

Former navy officer Cole Bishop returns to Serendipity, Texas, to raise his new baby—not to fall in love. But reconnecting with his high school sweetheart could be this hunky cowboy's chance to have it all.

RANCHER DADDY
Family Ties • by Lois Richer

Rancher Luc Cramer has always wanted children. As Holly Janzen helps him with the adoption process, can he come to terms with his troubled past and realize the caring nurse is the ideal mom for his new family?

FAMILY WANTED
Willow's Haven • by Renee Andrews

Isabella Gray feels an instant connection with widower Titus Jameson and his little girl. She's determined to help sweet Savannah come out of her shell, but will her handsome dad prove to be the strong, solid man Isabella's been searching for?

LOVING THE COUNTRY BOY
Barrett's Mill • by Mia Ross

Tessa Barrett moves to Barrett's Mill, Virginia, looking for a fresh start. Soon the city girl is falling for the small town's charm—and an easygoing country boy who's set on winning her heart.

NURSING THE SOLDIER'S HEART
Village of Hope • by Merrillee Whren

Army medic Brady Hewitt is eager to make up for lost time with his sick grandmother. After enlisting Village of Hope nurse Kirsten Bailey's aid, the pair realize that together they might just have a chance at happiness.

A FATHER'S SECOND CHANCE
by Mindy Obenhaus

Contractor Gage Purcell is the best candidate for Celeste Thompson's home renovations. But as she falls for the single dad and his two little girls, she begins to wonder if he's also the perfect man for her happily-ever-after.

LOOK FOR THESE AND OTHER LOVE INSPIRED BOOKS WHEREVER BOOKS ARE SOLD, INCLUDING MOST BOOKSTORES, SUPERMARKETS, DISCOUNT STORES AND DRUGSTORES.

LICNM0715

REQUEST YOUR FREE BOOKS!

2 FREE INSPIRATIONAL NOVELS
PLUS 2
FREE
MYSTERY GIFTS

Love Inspired®

YES! Please send me 2 FREE Love Inspired® novels and my 2 FREE mystery gifts (gifts are worth about $10). After receiving them, if I don't wish to receive any more books, I can return the shipping statement marked "cancel." If I don't cancel, I will receive 6 brand-new novels every month and be billed just $4.99 per book in the U.S. or $5.49 per book in Canada. That's a saving of at least 17% off the cover price. It's quite a bargain! Shipping and handling is just 50¢ per book in the U.S. and 75¢ per book in Canada.* I understand that accepting the 2 free books and gifts places me under no obligation to buy anything. I can always return a shipment and cancel at any time. Even if I never buy another book, the two free books and gifts are mine to keep forever.

105/305 IDN GH5P

Name _____ (PLEASE PRINT)

Address _____ Apt. #

City _____ State/Prov. _____ Zip/Postal Code

Signature (if under 18, a parent or guardian must sign)

Mail to the **Reader Service:**
IN U.S.A.: P.O. Box 1867, Buffalo, NY 14240-1867
IN CANADA: P.O. Box 609, Fort Erie, Ontario L2A 5X3

**Are you a subscriber to Love Inspired® books
and want to receive the larger-print edition?
Call 1-800-873-8635 or visit www.ReaderService.com.**

* Terms and prices subject to change without notice. Prices do not include applicable taxes. Sales tax applicable in N.Y. Canadian residents will be charged applicable taxes. Offer not valid in Quebec. This offer is limited to one order per household. Not valid for current subscribers to Love Inspired books. All orders subject to credit approval. Credit or debit balances in a customer's account(s) may be offset by any other outstanding balance owed by or to the customer. Please allow 4 to 6 weeks for delivery. Offer available while quantities last.

Your Privacy—The Reader Service is committed to protecting your privacy. Our Privacy Policy is available online at www.ReaderService.com or upon request from the Reader Service.

We make a portion of our mailing list available to reputable third parties that offer products we believe may interest you. If you prefer that we not exchange your name with third parties, or if you wish to clarify or modify your communication preferences, please visit us at www.ReaderService.com/consumerschoice or write to us at Reader Service Preference Service, P.O. Box 9062, Buffalo, NY 14240-9062. Include your complete name and address.

LI15

SPECIAL EXCERPT FROM

Love Inspired.

*Reuniting with her high school sweetheart is hard
enough for Tessa Applewhite, but how much worse will
it get when she realizes the newly returned cowboy has
brought with him a baby son?*

Read on for a sneak preview of **Deb Kastner**'s
THE COWBOY'S SURPRISE BABY,
the next heartwarming chapter in the series
COWBOY COUNTRY.

"So you'll be wrangling here," Tessa blurted out.

"Yep." His gaze narrowed even more.

Well, that was helpful. Tessa tried again.

"You've been discharged from the navy?"

He frowned and jammed his fists into the front pockets
of his worn blue jeans. "Yep."

She was beyond frustrated at his cold reception, but
she supposed she had it coming. She could hardly expect
better when the last time they'd seen each other was—

Well, there was no use dwelling on the past. If Cole
was going to work here with her, he would have to get
over it.

So, for that matter, would she.

"Well, I won't keep you," she said, reaching back to
open the office door. "I just wanted to make sure we had
an understanding about how our professional relationship
here at the ranch was going to go."

He scowled at the word *relationship*. "Just came as a
surprise, is all," he muttered.

"I'll say," Tessa agreed.

"Didn't expect to be back in Serendipity for a few years yet. Maybe ever."

He sounded so bitter that Tessa cringed. What had happened to the boy she'd once known? Who or what had darkened the sunshine that had once shone so brilliantly in his eyes?

"Cole? Why did you come back now?"

He tipped his hat and started to walk past her without speaking, and Tessa thought she'd pushed him too far. Whatever his issues were, clearly she was the last person on earth he'd talk to about them.

He was almost out the door when he suddenly swiveled around to face her.

"Grayson." His gaze narrowed on her as if weighing the effect of his words on her.

She scrambled to put his answer in some kind of context but came up with nothing.

"Who—"

He cut off her question and ground out the rest of his answer.

"My son."

Don't miss
THE COWBOY'S SURPRISE BABY by Deb Kastner,
available August 2015 wherever
Love Inspired® books and ebooks are sold.

"Alexandrina," James said, guiding his magnificent horses up a muddy, rutted trail that hardly did them justice. "That's an unusual name. Does it run in your family?"

She couldn't tell him the fiction she'd grown up hearing, that it had been her great-grandmother's name. "I don't believe so. I'm not overly fond of it."

He nodded as if he accepted that. "Then why not shorten it? You could go by Alex."

She sniffed, ducking away from an encroaching branch on one of the towering firs that grew everywhere around Seattle. "Certainly not. Alex is far too masculine."

The branch swept his shoulder, sending a fresh shower of drops to darken the brown wool. "Ann, then."

She shook her head. "Too simple."

"Rina?" He glanced her way and smiled.

Yes, he definitely knew the power of that smile. She could learn to love it. No, no, not love it. She was not here to fall in love but to teach impressionable minds. And a smile did not make the man. She must look to character, convictions.

"Rina," she said, testing the name on her tongue. She felt a smile forming. It had a nice sound to it, short, uncompromising. It fit the way she wanted to feel—certain of herself and her future. "I like it."

He shook his head. "And you blame me for failing to warn you. You should have warned me, ma'am."

Rina—yes, she was going to think of herself that way—felt her smile slipping. "Forgive me, Mr. Wallin. What have I done that would require a warning?"

"Your smile," he said with another shake of his head. "It could make a man go all weak at the knees."

His teasing nearly had the same effect, and she was afraid that was his intention. He seemed determined to make her like him, as if afraid she'd run back to Seattle otherwise. She refused to tell him she'd accepted his offer more from desperation than a desire to know him better. And she certainly had no intention of succumbing to his charm.

Don't miss
FRONTIER ENGAGEMENT by Regina Scott,
available August 2015 wherever
Love Inspired® Historical books and ebooks are sold.